JAMES PATTERSON
BOOKSHOTS

Dear Reader,

You're about to experience a revolution in reading—BookShots.

BookShots are a whole new kind of book—100 percent story-driven, no fluff, always under $5.

I've written or cowritten nearly all the BookShots and they're among my best novels of any length.

At 150 pages or fewer BookShots can be read in a night, on a commute, or even on your cell phone during breaks at work.

I hope you enjoy *Malicious*.

All my best,

James Patterson

P.S.

For special offers and the full list of BookShot titles, please go to: **BookShots.com**

BOOK**SHOTS**

Zoo 2 (with Max DiLallo) • *Cross Kill* (by James Patterson) • *The Trial* (with Maxine Paetro) • *Little Black Dress* (with Emily Raymond) • *The Witnesses* (with Brendan DuBois) • *Chase* (with Michael Ledwidge) • *Let's Play Make-Believe* (with James O. Born) • *Hunted* (with Andrew Holmes) • *Trump vs. Clinton* (Edited by James Patterson) • *113 Minutes* (with Max DiLallo) • *$10,000,000 Marriage Proposal* (with Hilary Liftin) • *French Kiss* (with Richard DiLallo) • *Taking the Titanic* (with Scott Slaven) • *Killer Chef* (with Jeffrey J. Keyes) • *Come and Get Us* (with Shan Serafin) • *Private: The Royals* (with Rees Jones) • *Black & Blue* (with Candice Fox) • *The Christmas Mystery* (with Richard DiLallo) • *The House Husband* (with Duane Swierczynski) • *Hidden* (with James O. Born) • *Malicious* (with James O. Born) • *French Twist* (with Richard DiLallo)

James Patterson's
BOOKSH⊙TS
Flames

Learning to Ride by Erin Knightley • *The McCullagh Inn in Maine* by Jen McLaughlin • *The Mating Season* by Laurie Horowitz • *Sacking the Quarterback* by Samantha Towle • *The Return* by Erin Knightley • *Bodyguard* by Jessica Linden • *Dazzling: The Diamond Trilogy, Book I* by Elizabeth Hayley • *Radiant: The Diamond Trilogy, Book II* by Elizabeth Hayley • *Hot Winter Nights* by Codi Gary • *Exquisite: The Diamond Trilogy, Book III* by Elizabeth Hayley • *A Wedding in Maine* by Jen McLaughlin

MALICIOUS

A MITCHUM STORY

JAMES PATTERSON
WITH JAMES O. BORN

BOOKSHOTS

Little, Brown and Company

New York Boston London

Copyright © 2017 by James Patterson

BookShots / Little, Brown and Company
Hachette Book Group
1290 Avenue of the Americas, New York, NY 10104
bookshots.com

First Edition: February 2017

BookShots is an imprint of Little, Brown and Company, a division of Hachette Book Group, Inc. The Little, Brown name and logo are trademarks of Hachette Book Group, Inc. The BookShots name and logo are trademarks of JBP Business, LLC.

The Hachette Speakers Bureau provides a wide range of authors for speaking events. To find out more, go to hachettespeakersbureau.com or call (866) 376-6591.

ISBN 978-0-316-50344-0
LCCN 2016943250

10 9 8 7 6 5 4 3 2

LSC-C

Printed in the United States of America

MALICIOUS

CHAPTER 1

I HAD RACED through my paper route this morning, chucking papers onto the frozen front yards of Marlboro, New York, in January. Normally, I'd stop and chat with the customers who happened to be up around dawn, but today I just waved. It's a shame, because that's my favorite part of the job.

Now I was in my unofficial office for my unofficial second job. For the past few years I had made my office in a little diner off Route 9 named Tina's Plentiful. Tina didn't mind, because I occasionally brought in a little extra traffic. I have to admit that lately there hadn't been much extra traffic. But right now, Edith Ledbetter sat across from me with a pleasant look on her aging face. No one under seventy is ever named Edith. She'd approached me about three months ago to see if I could locate her estranged daughter. They hadn't spoken in twenty-six years, since the daughter turned twenty-one and thought that Syracuse University had turned her into the smartest human on earth.

But years have a way of making people lonely and feel their regrets more acutely. Even after I explained that I wasn't a licensed private investigator, Edith said that she didn't care and hired me on the spot. Word-of-mouth recommendations in the community had helped me. I was honest and generally let my clients decide how much they wanted to pay.

We'd been waiting together almost forty-five minutes and there was no sign of the daughter. She had told me she would be at the diner at eight o'clock. I didn't like the looks of this at all.

Edith said, "It's some kind of miracle that you found Linda after all these years."

"All I really did was use the internet. It wasn't that big a deal."

"And you drove all the way down to Philadelphia." Edith looked up at the clock on the wall between the two framed posters of the California coastline. "Are you sure she really wanted to see me?"

I hoped Edith wasn't keeping track of the time.

"Of course she wants to see you." It was a shade of the truth. The daughter had been hesitant, but when I told her about the sweet eighty-year-old woman who missed her, she had agreed to meet at the diner when she was on a trip to Albany with her husband.

The new waitress, Alicia, flashed me a wide smile from

the counter. She was the only one here I had let in on the plan. Her intelligent eyes darted to the front door. She sensed my apprehension. I just shrugged.

Edith said, "Maybe she changed her mind. She's waited this long. I bet it was too much for her."

Alicia came by with some coffee for us and chatted with Edith about her homemade sweater and how nice her new glasses looked.

Alicia, God bless her, knew to keep Edith's mind off the time.

I said, "Edith, there could have been a mix-up. Although the roads are clear, it's awfully cold and it might've changed Linda's plans. Should we wait at your house where you might be more comfortable?"

"But what if Linda shows up and we're not here?"

I looked at Alicia, who was still standing right next to our booth, and said, "I bet I could talk Alicia into calling us if Linda comes later."

Alicia nodded. She had replaced Mabel, a young woman whose death was still a mystery and haunted me. I respected the fact that Alicia had moved back to Marlboro to care for her father while he recovered from a stroke.

Just as I got Edith to her feet and we turned toward the front, I noticed a woman in an expensive leather coat standing silently just inside the door. It took me a moment to realize it was the same woman I'd spoken to in Pennsylvania three weeks earlier. She just stared at us. That's when my anger melted away. This woman was scared.

As I held Edith by the arm, I felt her tense and knew that she had recognized her daughter even after two and a half decades. Edith took a tentative step forward. The few people in the diner didn't even realize what was happening, but Alicia did. She wrapped my hand in hers and squeezed it.

I watched in excited silence as Edith moved closer to her daughter. Suddenly Linda burst forward and hugged her mother. They both started to cry. So did Alicia. Damn it, so did I, but I was able to cover it well.

They both plopped down in the booth closest to where they'd been standing, holding each other's hands across the table.

Then my phone rang and I saw it was my brother, Natty.

I thought about ignoring the call. Now wasn't the time and Natty wasn't the person I wanted to talk to. I hate to confess it, but the scene made me really want to call my mom.

But guilt got the better of me and I answered the phone, "Hey, what's up?"

"I never thought I'd say this, but I need your help. I need your private investigator skills."

My brother wasn't much for compliments. I was skeptical and knew my brother could be a jackass. I always had to be on the lookout for pranks.

I said, "What kind of case?"

"A homicide. I'm not kidding, Mitchum, I need your help right now."

I looked up at Edith and her daughter, who were chatting like family should, and told Natty, "I'm on my way."

If there was one thing I knew about my brother, it was that he had a knack for making mistakes. And it seemed like this one was deadly.

CHAPTER 2

I DIDN'T GENERALLY look forward to seeing my brother at his place of business in Newburgh, about twenty-five minutes south of Marlboro. He worked out of a bar called the State of Mind Tavern that didn't seem to ever close. It was a dingy, one-story building that spanned a full block, with the parking lot on one side and a busy, industrial street on the other.

As I pulled my beat-up station wagon into the lot, I saw my brother standing by the back door talking to two other men. My brother is two years older than me and thin as a rail, mostly from a life of cigarettes, skipped meals, and little sleep. Despite resembling a sickly marathon runner, he's surprisingly tough. My theory is it has something to do with being a minor-league dope dealer in a tough town like Newburgh.

At the moment, though, he looked like he might be overmatched as he exchanged angry words with two guys. One was built like him and the other was a Hispanic guy who obviously spent way too much time in the gym; he had arms like legs.

I walked up casually, not wanting to give away my intentions. But I knew it might annoy my brother that I didn't look worried.

The big man turned and saw me and waved me toward the back door of the bar, saying, "Move on. This has nothing to do with you."

I noticed my brother had a bloody lip and a red splotch across his left cheek. That pissed me off. Generally, I was the only one allowed to pound on my brother once in a while.

I said, "Everything all right, Natty?"

"Does it look like everything's all right?"

I admired my brother's bravado in the face of adversity.

I said, "You guys think you could step away from my brother for a minute? Maybe we can talk about the issue." I was serious, even though I probably was coming across as a smart-ass.

The smaller guy, wiry like my brother, who I'd already determined was in charge, said, "Ain't nothing to discuss. Got nothing to do with you."

"Except, like I said, he's my brother. Mom expects to see him in one piece."

The wiry guy looked over his shoulder and said, "Manny, deal with this."

Everyone talks about how big guys are scary, but if you've

been in a couple of fights, you learned a few things about dealing with giant, angry people. I let this behemoth turn toward me and square off just so I could get an idea of his abilities. Usually, when you're that big, you don't bother to learn the subtleties of martial arts or boxing. This guy was no exception. He balled up both fists and took a wide stance in front of me. I could've played with him and made it look like I had real skills, but instead I used an old, simple trick. I lifted my left hand high in the air and watched his eyes follow it like a puppy watching a ball. Then I used my right leg like a punter and brought it up right between his legs. The big man crumpled onto the ground while he tried to suck in some air.

The wiry guy spun away from my brother and started to reach under his shirt. My brother shoved him hard toward me, and I lifted my elbow to catch him square in the chin. When he stumbled back onto the ground, I stepped over and found the small, cheap .380 automatic pistol he was reaching for. I dropped the magazine and ejected the round in the chamber. Then I threw the thing down hard on the street and was shocked to see it skip along the asphalt and drop into a drain. It was like I had scored a goal in hockey. Without thinking about it, I reached up and my brother gave me a high five. Just like when we were kids.

I helped the giant man with the sore crotch stand and then grabbed the wiry guy by the arm.

"You guys need to be on your way. You can talk to Natty some other time." Somehow, I knew the nice, rented Cadillac parked right next to us was theirs, and I opened the door and stuffed the big guy behind the wheel.

After a minute, when they slowly pulled out of the parking lot, my brother said, "Thanks, little brother."

"Friends of yours?"

"He's the guy I think committed that homicide I called you about."

CHAPTER 3

I WAITED UNTIL the two men had pulled away in the rented Cadillac, then turned to my brother and said, "Is that what you called me about?"

"No, something else."

"You aren't gonna tell me?"

"It's nothing. Business dispute. No big deal."

"Who in the hell were they?"

Natty was rubbing his face where the big man had slapped him. "One of 'em is Alton Beatty, my competition and the main suspect in the homicide I called you about."

"Who's dead? I mean, aside from the usual homicide victims that pile up here in Newburgh."

The way Natty hesitated made me realize the case really did mean something to him. Maybe it'd mean something to me as well.

Natty said, "Pete Stahl was shot and killed on Friday."

I cocked my head. "Petey Stahl from Highland Middle School?"

"The same."

I felt my legs go a little weak and leaned on the hood of an old Dodge. "I haven't talked to him in a few months, but seriously? I really like that guy. Even though he became a…"

"Drug dealer?"

"I'm sorry, Natty, I didn't mean it like that."

Natty said, "I know." Then he surprised me by putting his arm around my shoulder.

Petey was a year older than my brother and three years ahead of me, but I remembered him as a decent football player and one of my brother's few friends who didn't pick on me too much. When I got out of the Navy, we would play basketball and complain about my brother.

"Does mom know?"

"Yeah, she's the one who suggested I call you. She and Pete's mom talk all the time and his mom is heartbroken. Not just because he was killed, but because no one seems to care. The police aren't even doing anything about it."

I thought about the boy I knew and the man who still seemed like a decent guy, no matter what he did for a living. Now he was dead.

Natty said, "He was a good friend and a good business associate."

I shook my head and said, "You mean dope dealer? At least call it by its name. I understand what you do, but I don't like it."

"Jeez, Mitchum, this isn't the 1970s. No one calls it dope anymore. That's insulting to our customers. We *enhance recreational activities*. Or, if you have to label us, you can say 'drug dealer,' but the word *dope* is offensive."

"So why is Alton Beatty a 'competitor' and Pete Stahl an 'associate'?"

"Because Alton is overly ambitious. That's why I think he killed Pete. They both focus more on meth and some of the more synthetic stuff, and the rumor was they made a big score in the city about a month ago."

"What kind of score?"

"Money and maybe something else. Sounded like some kind of recipe for a variation of meth. I know there's some Canadian dudes who're really interested in it and would pay big money to have it."

I was still wrapping my head around the fact that a kid I used to play football with was dead. This was tough to swallow and started me thinking about how it could've been Natty. I saw Pete's mom every once in a while and knew I wouldn't be able to face her if I didn't get involved. More than that, I had to give her some closure.

Natty said, "There's one other thing I should tell you."

"What's that?"

"You know how Pete was married?"

"Yeah, but I never met her."

"She's a beautiful girl named Katie. She wasn't involved in his business and still doesn't know exactly what he did for a living."

"Yeah, so?"

Natty said, "I think I'm in love with her."

CHAPTER 4

THE FIRST THING I wanted to do was get a look at the scene of the murder. That also got me away from the bar where my brother did business. His life depressed me.

I knew the streets of Newburgh pretty well because I'd lived in Marlboro most of my life. Newburgh is a bigger town that is visually interesting, with grand brick buildings and a downtown that could've been a background for movies about small-town America.

Now the city has seen some rough times and the only neighborhoods that are livable, at least if you have kids, are in the suburbs. The three-story brownstones have blue tarps on the roofs and duct tape patching cracks in the windows.

Route 9 or, as we call it in the city, South Robinson Avenue, weaves through a mixture of industrial, commercial, and residential areas that no longer give the impression of a prosperous city.

Natty told me Pete had been shot Friday night in front of a well-known drug house on North Miller Street near

Farrington Street. It was just a block east of Downing Park, which covered a little bit of the inner city in a blanket of green peppered with some baseball fields. I guess you could call it their version of Central Park.

My ten-year-old station wagon, with its shocks that'd been worn out from carrying bundles of newspapers in the back all the time, sounded like an old diesel trawler as I put-tered through the city. I parked more than a block away so I wouldn't attract attention.

Two boys, around six, with a small black dog stared at me as I stepped out of the car. I smiled and said, "Hey, boys."

As I stepped onto the sidewalk, their dog trotted over to me and started sniffing my leg. "He smells my dog on me."

"Where's your dog?"

I thought about Bart Simpson, my mutt, who preferred the heat of my house to the winter wind, and said, "My house."

"Why do you have a dog if you don't bring him with you?"

"That is a good point and I'll remember it."

As I walked along the uneven sidewalk, I noticed several sets of eyes on me and reached in my pocket to feel the familiar weight of my commemorative Navy knife with a combat blade. Generally, I only use it to open boxes and cut the straps on bundles of papers, but I *had* used it to de-fend myself. I briefly thought about my Beretta back at the house, but I was never one of those guys who felt like he needed to carry a gun all the time. That's how a place like this city got to be a place like this city.

The spot where Pete died was on the steps of a three-story brick brownstone that looked abandoned. The vacant lot next to it had been used as a dumping ground for God knew how long. Plastic bags were stuck on the sagging chain-link fence and piles of trash blew all over the lot. An old pickup truck rusted near the back fence.

A line of young men on the porch of the house next door watched me. Despite the cold, a couple of them sat on a sagging couch wearing nothing but wifebeater undershirts. They were showing off how tough they were.

I had to shake my head and mutter, "Idiots."

There was still evidence of the crime scene right on the steps leading up to the front door of the house. I saw pieces of police tape, and the dark stain on two of the steps had to be blood. No one bothered to clean places like this very thoroughly after a murder. It was the same everywhere. Only this was a place where someone I knew had died.

I crouched down to examine the stain and looked up to see if I could figure out what had happened. The little I had learned on the internet about the shooting said that Pete was unarmed and stumbled onto the stairs with two gunshot wounds to his abdomen. At the time, people had been renting the house, but they had all fled the night of the shooting. It had been nothing but a drug house for the past decade, and no one seemed to be able to do anything about it. The whole situation made me ashamed of my brother and how he made a living.

As I crouched there, drawing the attention of the neighbors, a dark-blue Ford Crown Victoria pulled to the curb directly in front of the house. All it needed was lights on the top to advertise it was a police car. I stood slowly and turned as the car door opened.

A big man, an inch taller than me with more meat on his shoulders, emerged from the car, looked at me, and said, "Hey, dropout, what do you think you're doing in the big city?"

CHAPTER 5

I STARED AT the Newburgh detective, who wore a heavy coat over a cheap shirt and tie, and remembered his name was Mike Tharpe. Last time I'd seen him, a few months ago, he'd also thought it was funny to call me "dropout." I guess it was true, I *had* dropped out of Navy SEAL training during my final week. But it wasn't exactly a decision on my part. Either way, I accepted my past. Now I needed some questions answered and I didn't need to antagonize a cop, especially if he was trying to jostle me.

As the detective stepped toward me, one of the men on the porch made a pretty good pig grunt. It carried across the open space. The men on the porch all started to laugh.

Tharpe looked up at the man who had made the noise and said, "You must've heard that last night from your mom when I was visiting. Sometimes she likes to make a sound like an elephant, too, ya know?" That sent an uncomfortable silence through the group. The man who had made the sound was clearly furious. It made no impact on the veteran Newburgh detective.

Tharpe looked at me and said, "If you're looking for your brother, he usually hangs out at a bar on South Robinson Street."

"You mean the State of Mind Tavern? I know. I talked to him a little while ago."

"What brings you here? I mean to this neighborhood."

"My brother said a friend of ours was killed here."

"You knew Peter Stahl?"

"He grew up in Marlboro." For some reason I didn't want this guy to know how much Pete meant to me. It was like he hadn't earned the right to know my pain. I said, "My brother told me what happened and I was curious about his murder."

"Murder! He died of natural causes."

I stared at the detective and said, "I read that he was shot to death."

"That *is* natural causes for a dope dealer."

"Drug dealer."

"What?"

"No one calls it dope anymore. They call themselves *drug* dealers." I usually didn't split hairs but did when it annoyed someone in a position of authority.

CHAPTER 6

THARPE SIGHED, THEN took a few minutes to explain what had happened. He led me toward the house, pointing through the open door into the hallway.

"Near as I can figure, one of the local dopers"—he paused and looked at me—"sorry, *drug dealers,* thought Stahl was moving in on his territory and made a business decision."

We climbed the five stone steps to the landing in front of the door. The men from next door were acting like we didn't exist, which was fine with me.

Once we were in the hallway, Tharpe looked at me and said, "Did you know Stahl well?"

I calculated my answer carefully. I shrugged my shoulders and said, "My brother says you guys aren't doing everything you could to solve the shooting."

Tharpe stiffened at that. "If I did everything I could on every shooting in this screwed-up town, I wouldn't have time to sleep." His face turned a little red. "Peter Stahl sold dope and got shot. It's the natural order of things. Happens all the time. That's what we call the 'price of doing business.'"

We stood in the door and looked out onto the street. Tharpe explained to me how Pete had stumbled out of the vacant lot next door before he fell onto the steps. He said, "Stahl had been shot twice at close range. No one heard the shots and only a couple of locals acknowledged the body. By the time the crime scene was secured and police arrived, the only evidence was a body on the steps and a pistol that was found in the lot. It's being examined, but there's no telling what they'll find, or when. Our backlog would blow your mind. One of our narcotics guys thinks it might have been Stahl's own gun." He looked out over the neighborhood. "I don't know why we try so hard. There were no casings recovered, no witness who claimed to have seen anything or heard the shots, and all we got was an anonymous call to 911."

I thought about the facts: gunshot death of a known drug dealer. No witnesses. There wasn't much I could do. The police had declared the death a homicide and the listed potential motive as drug-related activity. That was about as much work as the Newburgh police intended to put into the case. I knew I had to at least do something. I wasn't sure I could face Pete's mom or sisters otherwise. They needed to know that someone had looked at the case.

I listened as Tharpe explained what he thought happened and how the police responded. This time I asked him, "Did *you* know Pete?"

"Knew his name from my days in narcotics. Just another lowlife." He held up his hand and said, "No offense. I mean, about your brother."

"None taken. He *is* a lowlife. But he's also my brother, and Pete was my friend, so I'm going to help."

Tharpe turned and focused his full attention on me. He said, "Look, I'm a fellow vet. Did four years in the Marines. I'm telling you, you need to give up being everyone's unpaid private investigator. The Newburgh police are looking for veterans right now. We got some kind of grant to hire them. It's a decent job with a good retirement. No one will hold anything your brother has done against you. You'd like the feeling of camaraderie again."

I was surprised by the offer, and I'd be lying if I said I didn't consider it for a minute. My main career as a paperboy wasn't everything I'd hoped it would be. And with this new job, I'd still be able to live in Marlboro in my little house surrounded by all my family. But I knew this wasn't the time to give an answer.

As we started to walk back outside, Tharpe said, "Sure, there are some headaches on the job. You have to put up with punks and shits, but you also get to knock heads once in a while and do some good. You should think about it."

It was a charming offer, but I was never much for "knocking heads." And my experience told me that "punks" often matured into decent human beings. Of course, that experience mainly came from being in the Navy, which had a tendency to straighten people out.

Right now I wasn't interested in anything other than the person who killed my friend.

CHAPTER 7

I DIDN'T TELL Natty about my chat with Detective Tharpe as we drove in his new, leased Chevy Camaro to a nice area outside Newburgh close to Firthcliffe, in an upscale development. I wondered if any of Pete's neighbors had known what he did for a living. My bet was that he was smart enough to do business away from his home, especially since he'd been keeping his job from his wife, Katie. Apparently, she didn't even know what business Pete was involved in. Not all drug dealers show that kind of common sense.

As we pulled into the cul-de-sac where Pete Stahl had lived with Katie in a small, single-story house, Natty started acting weird, even weirder than usual. I had no idea what was going on inside that foggy brain of his, but I felt like he was holding something back from me. He clearly didn't feel like talking just yet. I suspected it had something to do with his feelings for Pete's widow.

We parked in the driveway behind a new BMW and I

noticed a woman standing at the front door. As I climbed out of Natty's low Camaro, I realized the woman was much younger than I thought she'd be, probably not yet twenty-five. Her loose blond hair, blowing in the breeze, made her look like the girl next door. The beautiful one. Her face lit up as soon as she saw Natty. She wore jeans and a bulky sweater and those crazy boots younger women tended to wear, the ones with the name like "Neanderthal."

Natty introduced us and she had good manners, smiling as she shook my hand and looked me in the eye. She said, "Thank you for helping us. The Newburgh police have been polite, but they showed no real interest in Pete's murder."

I hadn't realized that Natty had told her I was taking the case. I liked her direct approach.

She served us iced tea as we sat on the couch. I couldn't help but glance around at her collection of the Peanuts characters in all shapes and forms, from ceramic to stuffed. The place had a certain childlike warmth to it that I was sure came from her. Even though they didn't have any kids, there were stuffed animals lying around on chairs and her beagle lay quietly in the corner, wearing a homemade knitted sweater.

Katie noticed my interest in the surroundings and said, "I use the toys for my job. I work with kids and they like to play with stuffed animals."

She sat down on a plush chair across from me, and for the

first time I noticed her bloodshot eyes. She had been crying. Maybe it was a cumulative effect from the last few days. I felt her sense of loss.

It made me think how easy it is to write off shootings reported on the news. No matter who was killed—a drug dealer, a gang member, or some poor guy walking down the street who was hit by a stray bullet—they were someone's husband or child.

Katie said, "A detective talked to me on Saturday, but I could tell he was just going through the motions. I'm not stupid, I knew Pete was involved in some shady business, but we had an understanding. I didn't ask as long as he was careful. He also promised me he never hurt anyone. I know that our relationship wasn't perfect, but anything you could do to help find out who killed Pete would mean the world to me."

I said, "I'll do what I can, but right now there are absolutely no leads. I was hoping you might be able to tell me something about the night he was shot."

"No one could ever say Pete wasn't a hard worker. He was ambitious. He worked every Friday and Saturday night. It was one of the things that had driven us apart. I don't know what he was doing the night he was killed, but he usually wandered home around two or three in the morning. The Newburgh police came by and told me what had happened somewhere around one."

"Can you think of any reason someone would want to kill your husband?"

She just stared at me with those wide blue eyes and shook her head. "Pete was a great guy. No one wanted to hurt him."

She stood up and took our glasses into the kitchen. A few moments later, she was back and sat on the arm of the chair that Natty was sitting in. She draped her hand across his shoulder and gave him a hug and a kiss on the top of his head. It was a show of affection for comfort. But it was obvious.

Natty avoided eye contact with me as I got a clear picture of what was going on. This was not a one-sided relationship.

CHAPTER 8

MY BROTHER AND I were quiet on the ride back through town to his office. I couldn't help but notice the number of abandoned buildings downtown and the lack of effort to clean up any of the garbage along the street or in vacant lots. This place was an advertisement for the "broken window theory" of government.

When we were inside the State of Mind Tavern and seated at Natty's personal table, he turned to me and said, "There's probably some more you need to know about what's going on."

"No kidding." I just stared at my brother, who remained silent until I said, "I'm listening."

Natty looked around nervously. The bartender who doubled as his bodyguard was used to me by now and didn't pay too much attention to our conversations. Finally, Natty said, "Katie told me she loved me, too. I mean, um, we've developed sort of a relationship. You know what I'm saying."

"Since Pete was killed Friday night?"

"No, it's been going on for a little while. She mentioned to you how they had drifted apart."

"But you said you thought you loved her. Didn't you also say she was faithful to Pete?"

"That's true. It's just how we feel about each other. It's not like we've slept together. She's not that kind of girl."

I appreciated the fact that my brother could still surprise me. I considered his awkward confession and finally said, "You didn't have anything to do with Pete's murder, did you?"

Natty looked hurt. "Do you have to ask?"

"Yes, of course I do. Natty, you're a criminal by trade. You've got a thing for a guy's wife. If the cops knew this you would be their only suspect. So I have to ask if you killed Pete."

Natty looked down toward the table and shook his head. "No, I didn't kill Pete."

I leaned back in the chair, tipping it up on the rear two legs as I looked at my brother and decided I believed him completely. That didn't change the fact that his relationship with the widow of his friend and business associate wouldn't look good if word got out. Deep down I had a feeling I wouldn't express right now: I liked the idea of my brother interested in a nice girl like Katie who wasn't involved in a scam or part of his usual world.

As I was still considering this new information, the front door suddenly opened and the room filled with sunlight.

Mike Tharpe and another detective stepped in the doorway and made a quick scan of the bar. Tharpe walked toward us while his partner faced the bartender. I recognized the good tactical sense.

Tharpe kept standing as he looked at Natty and said, "You're under arrest. You want to make it easy or do you want to make it fun for me?"

I was the one who said, "What's the charge?"

The meaty detective didn't even glance at me. "Homicide. We got some forensics back on a weapon we recovered. It was Pete Stahl's gun."

I said, "So why does that make my brother a suspect?"

"His fingerprints were on it and we think the DNA we're testing now will come back to him. You wanted me to clear this up and this is how I'm doing it. Now you don't have to worry about finding out who killed your friend."

"You didn't know any of this earlier today when we were talking?"

"You made me realize I had to do something, and when I checked with the lab, this is what came back. I want to thank you for doing your civic duty and motivating me." He motioned for my brother to stand up and did a quick patdown, then handcuffed Natty behind his back. In the big scheme of things, it was a fairly civil interaction, considering my big brother was going to jail.

CHAPTER 9

AS THE TWO detectives led a handcuffed Natty out of the bar, he turned to the bartender and said, "Call Lise." Then he looked at me and said, "Don't worry, little brother. For once, I'm innocent."

I stepped to the door to watch them stick my brother in the back of a black Ford Crown Victoria. Apparently the Newburgh Police Department had gotten a pretty good deal on the model. I stayed on the curb until the Ford pulled down the street and out of sight.

The few people on the street didn't seem interested in a nonviolent arrest.

When I stepped back inside I said to the bartender, "Who's Lise?"

The surly bartender barely looked up from the ledger he was working on and said, "Best attorney this side of the city. She changed everything when she showed up last year. Natty is as good as out on this bullshit. I just called her and she said you can go by her office around five. She'll know something by then, after she talks to the DA."

That was more words than the bartender had ever spoken to me.

I debated calling my mom but wanted to have more information first, so I drove around Newburgh to get a better feel for the city. It had a bad reputation, but I had learned that cities, just like people, rarely matched the way they were portrayed in the media. Almost every other year, Newburgh was listed as the most dangerous city in New York or given some title like "Murder Capital of the State." And to be fair, it had been flooded with drugs, guns, and gangs, in that order. But there were a lot of people trying to make it a better place to live. People who understood that working with at-risk kids could have the biggest payoff down the road. I noticed adults coaching kids in every park and mothers keeping a close eye on their toddlers as they played. They were families, and that meant there was still hope for Newburgh.

I found the law office on Ann Street near downtown. The building was a typical three-story brick, block-shaped structure with a little grocery store stuck awkwardly to the side. Lise Mendez's office was on the second floor, and of course there was no elevator. The building housed a couple of lawyers, an accountant, and a financial planner. It was a drug dealer's dream. When I found the right door, there was no name painted on the glass, just a card taped in the corner. This did not instill confidence as I stepped into the room and realized the reception area was unused and empty except for a couple of chairs. I heard a voice in the inner office say, "In here."

I stepped through the door to find Lise Mendez standing behind a large, ornate desk that didn't seem to go with the office. She had a pretty face and long, black hair tied in a loose ponytail. She was probably thirty-five and radiated that sort of professional confidence that came from a good education and some success in her field.

She said, "You must be Nathaniel's brother." She extended her hand.

"I am." I glanced around to notice that her office, unlike the reception area, was packed with boxes and files, which to me was a good sign because it meant she was busy.

She said, "What's your name?"

"Mitchum."

"Your name is Mitchum?"

I didn't feel like explaining and I wanted to hear about my brother so I just said, "That's what everyone calls me." I glanced over at the wall nearest me and noticed her diploma. I looked at her and said, "Impressive, Harvard Law. Surprised you're not with one of the big firms in the city."

"I was, but I moved back here for family reasons." Now

she pulled Natty's file from a stack on her desk and motioned for me to sit down. I noticed my brother's file was pretty thick.

I said, "Natty called me to look into the death of his friend."

"Pete Stahl? I know. I represented him, too. Why did your brother ask *you* to look into it?"

"I'm sort of an unofficial private investigator and he…"

"Nathaniel told me you delivered papers."

"I do both." I decided I wanted to change the subject, fast. "Do I owe you any money for this yet?"

The pretty attorney shook her head and said, "No, your brother keeps me on retainer. Granted, it's normally for narcotics cases, but let's see what happens with this. So far all they have is the gun used to kill Pete, and unfortunately, Nathaniel's fingerprints and, potentially, his DNA are on the gun. There are no witnesses, nothing else."

"Do you believe Natty when he says he had nothing to do with it?"

"I don't have to believe him. I just have to make sure his rights aren't violated, and that means that I'll protect him. If he had nothing to do with the murder and I protect his rights, he'll be a free man soon enough."

"Have you handled many cases like this?"

"A few."

"How many defendants walked free?"

"Every single one who deserved to. This isn't a sporting event where you keep score. I'll do my best. If that isn't good enough, there are other attorneys in town."

I considered what she had said and nodded, then said, "Do you think they'll let me visit Natty tonight?"

"They usually don't at the police department holding cell, but probably when he gets to the county jail." She took a Post-it pad from the corner of her desk and wrote down the phone number for the jail in the western part of the county.

I took the single blue square sheet of paper with an upstate New York logo that said *Adirondacks are not only chairs*.

I looked back at her and said, "What can I do to help?"

"I don't need some half-assed PI on this. Sorry, no offense."

I gave her a quick smile to let her know I had a sense of humor, but said, "Offense taken."

CHAPTER 10

IT TOOK MUCH longer than I expected to get through the Newburgh police red tape and see my brother in his holding cell. First, I sat in a room at the front of the station for thirty minutes. Then they moved me back to a visitors' area near the holding cells.

I'm a big guy at six two and 190 pounds, yet all the Newburgh cops in uniform made me look like a scrawny teenager. I thought back to the offer of a job from Mike Tharpe. Maybe taking on that career would be more of a challenge than I assumed. I could see that the station was bustling. Newburgh in the winter. It was a wonderland.

While I was waiting at the counter by the holding cells, the policemen walked a few prisoners through the hallway behind the counter. Most of them looked like younger Hispanic men and I recognized some of the tattoos on their bodies that told me they might be gang members. Most walked quietly, but there were two that were barking the whole way and pushing back against the cop who was trying to lead them to their holding cell.

Finally, a middle-aged black man in a neat uniform with sergeant stripes stepped out of the hallway and behind the counter.

He said, "You Mitchum?"

"Yes, sir."

He broke into a genuine smile. Not one like the employee from the electric company gives you when you pay your bill. It made me like the guy instantly.

"My name is Bill Jeffries. Pleased to meet you." He stuck out his hand. This was the friendliest Newburgh cop I had ever met.

I shook his hand and said, "Do you think I can talk to my brother for a few minutes?"

"Normally you'd have to wait until he's booked at the county jail before you can visit him. We don't really have the facilities to allow face-to-face contact. But in your case I can make an exception."

I was starting to think Lise Mendez was one hell of an attorney. But then the cop said, "I know your mom, Elaine, from the hospital. She's a good lady and she's always talking about you boys. She's awfully proud of both of you."

"Even Natty?" I didn't mean for it to come out that way.

The man looked at me and put his hand on my shoulder.

"Son, one day you'll realize a good parent only knows pride. It takes a lot for any boy to alienate his mother."

I realized this guy had been around, but more important, he knew my mother pretty well. Either way, he was doing me a big favor and I appreciated it.

CHAPTER 11

SERGEANT JEFFRIES BROUGHT Natty out to me in the waiting area. He left him in handcuffs, but neither of us complained. I knew this meeting was a huge breach of protocol. He moved to the end of the counter to give us some privacy, which also made me wonder what his exact relationship with my mother was. It might make for an interesting conversation when I saw her later that night.

It wasn't the first time I'd seen Natty in custody. I know it isn't shocking to think a drug dealer might've been arrested more than once, and Natty had even done a ten-month stint in Ulster Correctional. Still, I didn't like looking at him in handcuffs.

Natty seemed calm enough as he said, "Did you get a chance to talk to Lise? What did she have to say? Will she be at my bail hearing in the morning?"

"She said she'll be there. She also said they recovered the

gun that was used to kill Pete and that they have your fingerprints and possibly your DNA on it."

Natty sat back, deep in thought. But he didn't deny it like I was hoping he would. Finally, he said, "I know I played with his 9mm at his house one afternoon. I was visiting Katie and he had left the gun on a dresser."

"Do you know how that will look? That's just not a good explanation for why your fingerprints were on the gun. Plus, no one will believe you weren't sleeping with her."

"It's a better explanation than me using it to shoot Pete."

"But that's the conclusion everyone will jump to. Especially after they discover you and Katie are involved. No one knows, right?"

"No. We were going to tell Pete about it soon and now she wants to wait a respectable amount of time before we take it to the next level or tell anyone. She's really upset about Pete, but their marriage was over a while ago."

"I don't understand it, Natty. I've never seen you googly-eyed over a woman before."

"Katie is different than any woman I've ever met. She could make me a better man. She's honest and decent. That's a lot to say about anyone. She's an occupational therapist who works with autistic kids. That's why she has all the stuffed animals around the house. I could see myself settling down with her."

"Would you keep your current career if you settle down and had kids?"

That made Natty think. Sometimes I wondered if my brother ever considered the future. He looked at me with total sincerity and said, "I think I'd like to try something else. The paramedics are all so nice to me and they do important work. I wonder how hard it would be to become a paramedic."

I let him consider his dream life for a little bit, then brought him back to reality. "What can I do to help you now? Is there anything you can think of that might have led to Pete's death?"

"Just his business with Alton. The stuff I already told you about. Alton Beatty isn't anything like he seems. That's a guy that might be able to provide answers. He just might not *want* to." Then Natty took my arm and said, "I'm not worried. I didn't do it and I have faith in Lise. But Katie won't move on until she knows exactly what happened to Pete. I need you to find Pete's killer for her. That's all that matters now."

CHAPTER 12

BY THE TIME I was back in Marlboro it was pitch-black outside and there was a light snow starting to fall. I don't know if it's because Marlboro is my hometown or that I was just glad to be out of Newburgh, but I felt a sense of relief when I pulled into my mother's driveway.

She still lived in the simple two-bedroom house where Natty and I grew up. She kept our bedroom the same so if either of us needed a place to stay we always had a bed. So far, I'd only taken her up on the offer a couple of times while I was on leave in the Navy. Natty had used the house to escape the police and avoid sticky situations with other drug dealers. I would hate to be the drug dealer who thought he could barge into my mother's house without her permission.

I knocked on the door as I opened it and called out, "Mom?" It's never a good idea to surprise my mom.

She stepped out from the kitchen and said, "Bill Jeffries already called me and caught me up on everything. He even worked it out for Natty to call me and managed to get your brother into a private cell at the county jail." She had a slight hitch in her voice, but was still her usual, efficient communicator. Then she said, "I talked to Pete's mother. She doesn't believe Natty had anything to do with it, either. I told her you'd figure it all out. She's been out of her head with grief. Pete's sisters stayed at the house around the clock to comfort her."

Then I noticed her eyes were red and I realized *she'd* been crying. That was not my mother. I had seen her mad plenty of times. That was terrifying. But I'd never seen her worried or sad before. I always assumed it was her training as a nurse. Natty or I would suffer some sort of injury like a broken arm and she'd talk to us like she was making lunch and never show emotion. This was unnerving.

She came out in the living room and gave me a hug. Then she said, "This is bullshit. They're just trying to clear a case quickly. Murder? No way. Not my Natty."

"But you had no problem believing the narcotics charges over the years."

"That was just business. I'd be a fool to think Natty wasn't a dope dealer."

"Drug dealer."

"What?"

"Nothing," I mumbled, realizing this wasn't the time to debate semantics.

My mom said, "I know exactly what Natty is. He sells

drugs for a living. Christ, he even tried to steal some OxyContin once when he visited me at the hospital."

I cringed, imagining what my mother had done to him. When she didn't offer any details, I had to say, "What did you do?"

"I tore that stupid earring he used to wear right out of his lobe."

The image was unsettling, but at least it solved a mystery. I had wondered why he had abruptly stopped wearing the earring. He also stayed down in Newburgh for a while after that. I guess so he had time for his ear to heal and he wouldn't have to answer a lot of questions.

My mom said, "No, my Natty would never kill anyone. He's basically a good boy."

That made me think about what Sergeant Jeffries had said about a parent's pride. I also thought about all the favors he'd done for Natty the last few hours, from getting him a private cell to allowing me to see him at the station. I blurted out, "Are you dating Bill Jeffries?"

Mom didn't hesitate. "Yes. Yes, I am."

I was a little shocked by her honesty. She had always kept her love life hidden from Natty and me. I just stood there, speechless.

She said, "Are you shocked I can attract a man?"

"No, not at all. It's just that I don't think about you and men. I mean, you are my mother."

"Are you too old to start calling someone Dad?"

"Yes. And besides, you were always both to me. A better mom and dad than any man could ever be."

My mom started to cry in front of me. Something I'd never seen. Then she gave me a hug. You're never too old to appreciate a hug from your mother.

CHAPTER 13

THE NEXT DAY, as soon as I finished my paper route, I headed to Tina's Plentiful for some breakfast and a place to think. Thank God my official booth was open, so I plopped down, already considering what I could do to help my brother.

The place was nearly empty this morning because snow was starting to build up on the roads. After a few minutes, while I was still lost in thought, Alicia placed a plate of eggs and ham in front of me and a bagel on the other side of the table. Then she slid into the booth.

Alicia said, "You look like you need some protein and company."

I smiled at her insight.

"You left so fast yesterday I didn't get a chance to tell you what a wonderful thing you did for Mrs. Ledbetter. She and her daughter stayed here an hour, then went back to her house. It was beautiful."

I gave her a smile. This was exactly the sort of thing I

needed this morning. Something light and friendly before I headed down to Newburgh.

Alicia said, "I get off just after lunch today. Are you free? Would you like to do something?"

My guess was that with a face like hers, she rarely had men turn her down. And I wanted to be here when she finished her shift. More than anything I could think of. But I thought of my brother sitting in the county jail and Pete Stahl's mom crying over her dead son, and I summoned the courage to shake my head.

"I'm sorry, Alicia. My brother's gotten into some hot water down in Newburgh and I couldn't face my mother again if I didn't do everything I could to help him."

"Your brother Natty, the drug dealer?"

Finally, someone was up on the current lingo for the job description. I nodded my head, still feeling the regret for turning down an offer to spend time with this beautiful girl.

"I hope you'll give me a chance to make it up to you as soon as I can. Maybe a nice dinner and movie up in Pough-keepsie."

She smiled and patted my hand. "You're a good brother and son. That's more important than an afternoon of wild sex."

My head snapped up at that. I smiled and said, "I wish you hadn't said that. Now that's all I'll be thinking about while I'm in Newburgh."

"That's okay. It was just a test to see how important your trip really was. You passed with flying colors. I'm very impressed."

A smile spread across my face as I realized just how smart and funny this girl was. Plus, I thought I could get lost in those brown eyes.

She grinned and said, "Eat up. You've got crimes to solve and brothers to rescue. Just remember your promise to take me out when this is all finished."

"Then, I'll have to find a way to clear this up right away."

CHAPTER 14

DRIVING THE STREETS of Newburgh, I wasn't really sure why I had rushed away from my breakfast with the beautiful girl who wanted to spend the afternoon with me. Snow did little to hide the deterioration of the city. All it did was keep more people inside and maybe a few cars off the road.

I spent a few minutes watching kids play a game of football in an open field. It was four on four and the two-hand touches were a little on the rough side. They were doing what kids did: having fun.

It made me think of Pete and the things we did and dreamed about as kids. He used to say he was going to be a sports trainer. Maybe work for the Buffalo Bills. We all had dreams. At least Pete realized he wasn't talented enough to play football professionally.

I never knew my limitations. I wanted to be a Navy SEAL. I thought I had all the bases covered. It turned out I'd missed one in order to get there.

I talked to a couple of people on the streets, using my cash sparingly to buy information. When you're a paperboy and a low-paid private investigator, there's no other way to use your cash but sparingly.

Each person led me to someone else who gave me a little more information. I wasn't being particularly discreet, but I was starting to get a clear picture of the drug trade in Newburgh.

Finally, later in the afternoon, I pulled up to a bar named the Budstop. This was where Alton Beatty ran his business, which apparently wasn't much of a secret in Newburgh.

I took a second to survey the building and parking lot. It didn't look that much different than the bar where my brother worked. I did notice the rented Cadillac in the parking lot and three pickup trucks parked directly in front of the building on the street. I wondered if that had something to do with Alton selling more meth than pot and cocaine.

I waited until all three trucks pulled away from the bar. All three of the drivers, who came out a few minutes after one another, looked like sickly rednecks. They were thin with sallow complexions. I don't know much about methamphetamine, but these guys looked like billboards designed to scare kids away from it.

I parked at the far end of the lot and came into the pub from the side door. I've never been much of a bar guy, and this place looked just like the State of Mind Tavern: dark and musty, and no place to be on a crisp winter day.

After I walked inside, it took a few seconds for my eyes to adjust to the lighting. When the room came into better focus, the big Hispanic guy I had kicked in the crotch was striding toward me from across the room. At least he wasn't reaching for a weapon. That proved that he had some brains.

He said, "You and me got some unfinished business." His voice sounded like a tuba.

I said, "I'm pretty satisfied with our last transaction. Are your balls still swollen?" I have no idea why I threw that last comment into the conversation. Or why I felt like I had to smile at him. It only pissed him off like I knew it would.

He squared off in front of me again. Not much different than he did the first time.

Today I had another test of his abilities in mind. I raised my left hand, just like I had during our first meeting. This time he didn't take the bait and kept his eyes on me and his big hands near his groin.

This was another old trick I had learned. I just balled my left fist and hit him with a wild haymaker across his chin. It was spectacular. I felt his jaw shift and his head snap to the side as he staggered backward, finally plopping into a chair next to an empty table.

Then the bartender and a sturdy-looking guy at a table

sprang into action. I saw a flash of metal and realized the bartender had a knife. I didn't have time to reach into my pocket and draw my commemorative Navy knife. I angled my body to give him the smallest possible target and got ready to show some Navy pride.

Then I heard a shout.

"Cool it, everyone."

CHAPTER 15

THE MEN FROZE as Alton Beatty stepped into the room from a rear hallway. He had his long hair in a ponytail and was wearing a simple plaid shirt and jeans. He hardly looked the part of the successful drug dealer.

Both the men froze but didn't retreat at Alton's command. As he stepped closer to me he said, "Jerry, Blade, step back."

I looked at the bartender and said, "Are you Blade?"

He smiled and nodded.

In my experience, a guy usually didn't get a nickname like Blade for no reason. He stepped back to the bar and I breathed a sigh of relief.

Now Alton Beatty was right in front of me. He said, "In all the time I've known Natty, he never mentioned he had a brother."

"I don't brag much about him, either."

"I hear you been askin' about Pete Stahl. Mind telling me why?"

I really noticed his twang in simple conversation. "Where are you from? I mean, originally."

"Outside Cincinnati."

"For some reason I thought you were from New York City."

"I went to NYU and stayed after graduation. I moved here from the city a couple of years ago."

"Excuse me. NYU? Are you kidding me?"

Alton gave me a smile of pride and said, "School of Business." He sharpened his gaze at me and said, "That's just your New York prejudice. Hear a slightly Southern accent and assume a person's stupid. I try to use it to my advantage."

"How did you get into drug dealing after graduating from NYU?"

"Easiest way to learn the metric system," he said, giving me a sly smile.

I looked around the seedy bar and said, "This place is just like the bar my brother works out of."

"You gotta go where the customers are. It's just smart business."

"Like killing Pete Stahl?"

"Don't be a dumbass. I worked with Pete. If you're gonna start throwing around accusations like that, I'll just refer you to my attorney, Lise Mendez."

"Jesus, she the only attorney in town?"

"Only one worth a shit, and who looks like that." He stepped closer to me and put his arm around my shoulder. "Speaking of beauties, how's Pete's wife, Katie? Is your brother still sniffing around her?"

CHAPTER 16

ALTON DIDN'T TELL me a whole lot, and his condescending attitude made me realize it was time to move on. At least for now. It was late afternoon by the time I left the Budstop. Dusk comes awfully early in upstate New York in winter. Especially with the low clouds that threatened more snow. The temperature dropped and I wasn't prepared for it. I stepped out of the side door and felt the sharp wind. There was ice across the parking lot, so I made my way as quickly as I could without losing my footing.

Alton hadn't given me the impression that he was a cold-blooded killer. But greed could do crazy things to people. I still had a lot of questions to ask and work to do.

I was lost in thought and concentrating on not falling, so I wasn't paying attention to my surroundings. That's a mistake in most circumstances and an all-out blunder when you're investigating a criminal case. I hadn't noticed anyone else in the parking lot before the man in the ski mask stepped out from behind my car.

I skidded to a stop, astonished. It was a big guy wearing a thick winter jacket. He didn't say a word as I just stared at him. Then he moved his right hand and I saw he had a red crowbar in it. It almost looked like a fireman's tool, but I knew he wasn't here to fight a fire.

I'd like to say I was prepared to fight him, but I was no idiot. My training in the Navy and specifically the SEAL class taught me when to evade. This was one of those times. I quickly spun and intended to dart back into the bar, when I felt the hook of the crowbar around my ankle, tripping me on my first step. I fell to the hard, icy asphalt and immediately rolled to my side, just as a blow struck the pavement where I had been lying.

I was able to scramble forward and gain my footing, but now I was facing my attacker and I didn't have an easy way to run. He stepped forward with confidence because he was wearing decent boots. I feinted left, then tried to jump to my right. The attacker fell for it at first, and swung the crowbar wildly as I tried to slip past him.

It caught my forehead with a glancing blow, opening up a gash. Almost immediately blood started to run down my forehead into my eyes. I took a second to wipe it with my sleeve and before I was finished, the attacker was on me again with the crowbar over his head. This time I jumped back and rolled over the hood of a newer Chevy.

As the attacker swung down with his crowbar, I slid off

the hood, and the curved part of the crowbar punctured the metal, locking the attacker's weapon in place. I knew this was my one chance so I kicked hard, catching the ski-masked man on his left side and knocking him to the ground.

It was a good, solid kick and the only thing that protected him was his padded jacket. I rushed forward, trying to take advantage of my good luck.

The man was able to fend me off and send me slipping back onto the icy asphalt. Then he turned and started to run across the street and out of sight.

I sat there for a minute, catching my breath and assessing my injury. As I stood up, holding my forehead, I noticed a Newburgh police cruiser pulling into the parking lot.

They were a little late, but I was still happy to see them.

CHAPTER 17

THE DRIVER OF the patrol car was a huge, bald black man, and his partner was a scrawny white guy with an odd-looking mustache that tilted at an angle to the right side of his face. They kept their distance as they asked a few questions and the white guy handed me some gauze to put on my forehead.

The black officer said, "We had a complaint about a disturbance in the area. You fit the description of the assailant pretty well."

"Assailant! I'm the victim. Can't you see this blood?"

"There's no law that says a victim can't kick an assailant's ass once in a while. Why don't you come with us and we'll straighten this out?"

"Come where?"

"To our station. There's someone there who wants to talk to you."

"But I…"

The big cop grabbed me by the arm and spun me. I could

have resisted. He was strong, but I was fast and better trained. No way I wanted to hurt a cop. Especially one who was just doing his job. I felt handcuffs across my wrist almost instantly.

He said, "You have the right to remain silent and I hope you have the ability to remain silent for your own good."

Ten minutes later, I found myself in a holding cell in the same area where my brother had been the night before. I understood what the big black cop had meant when he told me to keep quiet. There's a time to be a smart-ass and a time to shut your trap and listen. So far I hadn't heard anything of value, but I hadn't antagonized anyone, either. That was sort of new for me. I was starting to think these two cops were working outside their job description.

When they dumped me in the cell and took the cuffs off, the cop said, "Someone will be here in a few minutes to talk to you. I suggest you listen up."

Then I found myself alone on a hard bench, confused about what the hell had just happened.

I sprang upright on my bench when I heard the lock on my cell turn about fifteen minutes later. I wondered if these cops were bold enough to give me a beating right here in the cell. My whole body tensed at the idea.

At least the gash in my head had stopped bleeding; one of the cops had given me a Band-Aid for it. A big Band-Aid. I considered rushing whoever came in the door and trying to escape. But I knew no one would ever buy the idea that I was arrested on bullshit charges. Come to think of it, I hadn't actually been arrested. I guess you'd call it *taken into custody*. That started me thinking about why I'd really been picked out like this. *Could there be a rat in the police?*

I felt myself lift off the seat slightly, getting ready to charge. But when the door opened my whole body relaxed back onto the bench. Standing in the doorway was my mom's friend, Sergeant Bill Jeffries.

The sergeant gave me a smile and shook his head. "You Mitchum boys have stirred up a lot of shit in the last couple of days here in Newburgh."

"Are you the man I'm supposed to talk to?"

Sergeant Jeffries shook his head and motioned me to follow him. There were no handcuffs or searches involved as we hustled down the hallway. He led me through a door, which took us outside. He pointed to a cruiser and said, "Jump in the passenger seat."

I didn't ask any questions but could tell he was headed back toward the Budstop, where my car was parked.

Sergeant Jeffries said, "I don't exactly know what's going on here. You weren't officially booked. I'm not asking any questions about it, but you've made some enemies in the Newburgh police department. You need to get out of Newburgh and stay away from this case. Let your brother's lawyer do what she's good at."

"Come on, Bill. You know my mom. You think she'd let me drop this case?"

The sergeant chuckled and said, "Then you better start watching your ass more closely. There are a lot of bad people in this town."

CHAPTER 18

BEFORE SERGEANT JEFFRIES even dropped me off at my car at the Budstop, my phone rang. I was surprised to hear Katie Stahl asking me to meet her. I raced through Newburgh, or, at least, drove as quickly as I could in my beat-up station wagon, to where Katie had told me she was waiting: Lise Mendez's office.

As I stepped through the front door, Lise called from her office, telling me to come in.

As soon as she saw me, Lise said, "Is everything all right? What happened to your head?"

My hand rose to the giant Band-Aid on my forehead and reminded me I still had a slight headache. "Just clumsy."

Katie smiled and patted the chair next to her. "We need your signature on a couple of forms for Natty."

"What kind of forms?"

"I'm moving the retainer Pete had with Miss Mendez over to cover some of the expenses for Natty," Katie said. "She wanted to make sure there was no question if anyone asked where the money came from. I'm also trying to get a fix on my cash situation in case Natty gets a bond hearing so I can help him out."

Lise said, "There are a couple of businessmen in town that will help with Natty's bond as well. He's very well respected here in Newburgh."

"By businessmen, do you mean drug dealers?"

"Does it matter?"

I thought about it and shrugged. I couldn't believe how lucky my brother was to have two people like these women in his life. An attorney who was going above and beyond the call of duty and a young woman who trusted him enough to post a bond on a homicide charge. Whatever choices my brother made, he was doing all right in at least one department.

I filled out the paperwork and chatted with the women for a few minutes. Katie stood, slipped on a cute leather jacket, and got ready to leave.

The manners my mother had beaten into my brother and me demanded that I stand as well.

She gave me a quick hug. "Thank you for everything you're doing."

"I really haven't accomplished anything yet. But I'm not giving up." I didn't tell her that now I was prepared to take drastic measures to help my brother and find my friend's killer. You can only put up with bullshit for so long, and I was at my limit.

Once Katie had left, Lise looked at me and said, "I thought I said I didn't need any help on your brother's case."

"I'm not doing it for you."

She shook her head and looked down. "I hope to make some progress at the evidentiary hearing scheduled for next week. If the gun gets thrown out for any reason, your brother will be free to go."

I leaned in and said, "I heard you represent all the drug dealers in town."

"Why does that matter?"

"Because you represent my brother, Pete, and Alton Beatty."

"Alton has me on retainer. But that's really all I can say. Why? Is there something I need to know?"

"Did Pete or Alton ever tell you about some kind of big score they made in the city?"

"As I said, ethically, I can't tell you anything a client has discussed with me. That being said, typically, my clients don't call me unless there is some kind of problem. I don't hear about the successful business transactions."

I thought about how she could discuss this so casually and blurted out, "Does what you do for a living ever bother you?"

"You mean upholding people's rights?"

"I mean figure out ways for felons to get back out on the streets."

Lise said, "Like your brother?"

She hit the target on that last comment. I had no real retort other than to bow my head and say, "Touché."

There was an awkward silence that one of us needed to break.

Lise said, "Natty told me you were in school to be a Navy SEAL. He said it was all you ever wanted to be. How does a SEAL recruit become a paperboy and PI?"

"I had all the skills. I could run. Was great with weapons. I took karate since I was eight so I knew how to move. There was just one thing I underestimated."

"What's that?"

"Swimming. I could swim, but not the way I needed to. Upstate New York is not the best environment to become a great swimmer."

"You didn't know that going in?"

"I thought I'd get better going through the school in San Diego. Turns out, with everything we had to do, I couldn't keep up. The instructors cut me slack because I could do everything else. That's how I made it until the end of the course. Ultimately, I had to give up that dream and make a new one. I wanted to help people. Contribute to society. That sort of nonsense." I gave her a smile. "That's why I became a PI. Paid or not."

Lise said, "Not that I'm interested, but what's your next move looking into Pete's death?"

"I didn't see Alton Beatty's car at the Budstop on my way over here, so I think I'm going to go get some rest and track him down early tomorrow afternoon. Maybe scare a few answers out of him."

"He's not the simple redneck he pretends to be."

"Neither am I."

Lise said, "Be careful out there. Newburgh is a dangerous place."

"You're the second person today who's told me that."

CHAPTER 19

WHEN I START to concentrate on a case like this, I often lose track of time. The only thing I remember to do is my paper route early in the morning. I got up before dawn, like I do every single day, and delivered my papers. I do it not only because I get a regular paycheck, but because I know that I'm the lifeline to a number of elderly residents around Marlboro. It makes me get up every morning. I like to say hello and chat for a few seconds if one of my customers happens to be outside. I needed a regular, uneventful morning like this.

By midday, I was back in Newburgh and looking for Alton Beatty. The condescending little turd needed to have some answers for me or this would be an unpleasant day. It didn't take long to track down his Cadillac in the parking lot of the Budstop.

By now I had switched modes completely. I wasn't only a private investigator, I was the brother of a guy falsely accused of murder. My mom was depending on me. That meant something. At least to me.

I stepped through the side door of the bar. I didn't see the big bodyguard, but Blade's head snapped up as soon as I came into view. Alton was sitting in a booth reading a *New York Times.* He hopped to his feet as soon as he saw me.

He said, "Don't you know that it isn't polite to drop by without calling first? You Yankees sure don't have the manners of us folks from the Midwest. Why are you bothering me again? I told you everything I knew yesterday."

I glanced around the room quickly and noted that Blade stepped around the bar, ready to take action. "Where's your big bodyguard?"

"At the doctor having his fractured jaw fixed. I ought to bill you for the damage."

"Or invest in a better bodyguard."

"You're wasting my time, Mitchum. I got things to do. What do you want?"

"Let's say I believe you didn't kill Pete Stahl. You've gotta have an idea who did."

"You asking me as the town genius or as someone involved in the industry?"

"I didn't realize you were a genius."

"Not everyone does. Usually I call those people idiots. I'm guessing you went to a state school of some kind."

"I'm asking if you heard anything in your position as a local drug dealer."

"You trying to insult me? It sounds like you're talking

down to me. Frankly, you're not smart enough to talk down to me. No one is. I don't appreciate that sort of attitude in my business."

That was one sentence too many from this little prick. "Do you appreciate this?" I grabbed him by the collar of his shirt and pulled him close to me. "My brother is in deep shit for something he didn't do. I think you have information that can help me clear him. And you're gonna start talking. Right. Fucking. Now."

As soon as I released him, Alton took a step away and reached behind his back. Before I had time to act, he was holding a small semiautomatic pistol. Worse, he still had a smirk on his face as if he was absolutely brilliant for walking around with a gun.

I didn't hesitate. That's the key in a situation like this. I used my right hand to slap him hard across the face and at the same time grabbed the gun with my left hand. I twisted Alton's arm, pulling him close to me as I put the gun to his head. We shuffled toward the rear door. I looked at Blade the bartender and said, "Be cool and this will all work out. I don't think you want to blow your meal ticket just yet." As soon as we were outside, I pushed him forward into a brick wall that hid the dumpster.

I said, "I'm out of patience with you. You're gonna start talking or I'm gonna smack you around so hard no one in this town will ever respect you again. They'll have to take you by the emergency room to get this gun removed from your ass."

"You think because you're a big guy and were in the Navy that you know what tough is. Try being the smartest kid in Cincinnati who's only five foot seven. There's nothing you can do to me that will make me talk."

I didn't understand how a guy was so smart and still didn't understand the physics of a pistol. I shoved him up hard against the wall with my left hand under his chin, lifting him onto his tiptoes. Then I screwed the nozzle of the gun into his nostril.

He gave me a hard stare like he didn't think I had the nerve to pull the trigger.

I extended my thumb up and pulled back the hammer of the pistol, so he would hear the cocking sound and see the movement. That did it.

"Okay, okay, hang on one second."

I didn't move. I growled, "Talk."

And he talked quickly.

"Pete and I stumbled onto a new recipe for meth. One of the chemical engineering students from Columbia I used to buy shit from made it. We interrupted his deal with some Canadians and got lucky."

"How lucky did you get?"

Alton said, "Six hundred and fifty thousand."

"How much is the recipe worth?"

"We've been offered a million bucks for it. The Canadian mob is all over this. The Canucks love prescription pills and meth. And this recipe has them drooling."

"Why? What's so special about it?"

"You can make it with ingredients that aren't too hard to find. Not quite as potent, but it can be made on a big scale."

"Who has it?" The whole time he'd been talking I had been releasing my grip slightly, at least to the point where his feet were flat on the ground. Now I stepped back with the pistol still pointed at his face.

Alton was out of breath and sweating as he said, "Pete and I stashed the money and the recipe with the help of another partner. We wanted to make it so not one of us could get to the cash without the other two. It's in a bank up in Poughkeepsie and you need two keys to get into the box, and a code to get into the safety-deposit-box room without any questions."

"What do *you* have?"

Alton stuck his left hand into the front pocket of his jeans and pulled out a flat metal key with a number 68 on it. He said, "Pete had the other key, but I suspect whoever shot him took it."

I stared at the key.

Sensing my interest, Alton closed his fist around it and held it by his side.

I said, "You think I won't take it?"

"You'll have to kill me first. I earned this."

I decided to let it go for the moment. I said, "So who has the code?"

"Forget that. What you need to do is find out who has Pete's key. Whoever has the key probably killed Pete and has the answers to get your brother out of jail."

"I need some direction. You were my best lead."

"A cop picked up Pete on some cheap, narco charge. Pete told me—"

But that's when I heard the first gunshot.

CHAPTER 20

I DUCKED AT the first sound of the gunfire, then rolled to my right when I felt pieces of brick start to fly from the ricochets. I had Alton's little popgun in my hand and brought it up to fire a couple of times.

Alton was on the ground, so I grabbed him by the back of the shirt to pull him out of the line of fire and to cover. As soon as I grabbed his belt, his whole body went limp. As I brought him closer to me, I saw the bullet wound that went in through his cheek and exited the back of his head. His open eyes were already glassy.

Something shiny on the ground caught my attention. The key! I reached forward, trying to stay behind cover. A bullet pinged off the dumpster next to my extended hand. I lurched back. I stuck Alton's pistol around the dumpster and fired once to get the shooter's head down. Then I snatched the key and jammed it in my pocket as I tumbled back behind cover.

I caught a glimpse of someone in a dark coat running

between cars in the parking lot. I left Alton where he was and started to give chase. I could tell it was a male who was pretty big and, most important, still had the pistol in his hand. As he came out on the street, he turned to see if anyone was following him, and I dove onto the asphalt parking lot.

I was up again and running after a few seconds. I needed this guy. He could answer a lot of questions.

Now I was moving across the sidewalk in an all-out sprint. There was a little ice, but at this point I didn't care. There was no one who could outrun me when I was determined.

I took a corner hard, sliding out onto the road and narrowly missing a woman holding two kids by the hand. The woman gave a short shriek of surprise.

The little boy, in a dark-blue tattered parka, pointed down the street.

I gave him a nod of thanks and kept running. As soon as I came to the next block, I glimpsed the man at the edge of an industrial park. He turned and fired two more shots at me.

At this distance they both went wide, so I stayed in pursuit. When I was a little closer, I raised Alton's tiny pistol and popped off a round to keep the guy off balance.

Then I tried to do what the running man wouldn't expect. Instead of going right to where he was the last time I saw him, I cut into the industrial park and started to circle the building in between us. It was a little trickier here because there were workers coming and going in vans, carrying everything from windowsills to sprinkler pipes.

As I darted around the building, I saw what I needed to see. The guy with the gun was crouched behind a parked van, waiting to ambush me from the other direction. Perfect.

I eased into a line of cars so it wouldn't be easy for him to notice me. I wanted to say something clever like "Looking for me, asshole?" But I knew the most important thing was to get the pistol away from him.

When I was still a decent distance away, the man glanced over his shoulder. All I could tell from that angle was that he was a white man. I couldn't identify him specifically. Right now, that didn't matter. He turned and aimed his gun at me as I ducked behind a parked Honda Civic.

The two shots shattered the rear window of the car and made me crawl back farther away from the trunk. Then I heard a police siren.

I had to catch this guy now and get some answers before he was taken into custody.

I squeezed between some parked cars and crawled under one of them until I was close to the place where the man had taken the shots at me. I sprang out with the pistol up in front of me. There was no one there.

I could see the blue lights of the cruiser and I knew it was time to get the hell out of there.

CHAPTER 21

I DROVE TO a McDonald's on the outskirts of Newburgh's downtown. If you ever want good insight into a city, look through the wide windows of a Mickey D's. You see everything. The locals, workers from businesses, and the homeless. This intersection can provide a glimpse into the city's soul. Is it prosperous? Is it a college town? Or is it struggling, ready to chew you up and spit you out?

As I sat in the hard plastic booth, throwing down a hamburger and staring at the key I'd taken from Alton, my mom called. I worked hard to keep my voice calm as I told her there wasn't really anything new on the case. When I was in the Navy and going through the SEAL course, I always tried to paint the best picture. My mom worried about me. At least now, my job was to make her life as easy as possible.

About an hour after my chase through the streets of Newburgh, I decided it was safe to make my next move.

I walked through the front doors of the Newburgh

Police Department, leaned in close to the little circle cut into the thick, bulletproof glass, and asked the receptionist if I could speak to Sergeant Bill Jeffries.

I followed him through the bowels of the police station. He kept quiet. Seemed he was worried about people eavesdropping.

Once in his cramped office, I spun him my somewhat vague story about Alton Beatty and his relationship to Pete Stahl. I didn't give too many details because I still wasn't sure I could trust him.

Finally, he said, "The Alton Beatty you're talking about is the guy who was just shot at the Budstop about an hour ago, right?"

"Exactly."

"And you wouldn't know anything about a shoot-out between two men that lasted for several blocks?"

"Not a thing."

"Unfortunately, the only description of the two men shooting is that they were white males. Not a lot to go on."

I kept my expression blank.

Jeffries said, "Look, Mitchum, I know you had nothing to do with either death. I even know your brother didn't kill Pete Stahl. But there's a lot of weird shit going on. I don't get the sense that you're telling me everything."

"Maybe that's more for your own good than mine."

Jeffries nodded. He turned and typed on a keyboard. He

studied the screen, frowning as he scrolled through a few pages.

He said, "As the administrative sergeant, I can get into any part of our network. It looks like your friend Pete Stahl was arrested about a month ago but never booked. When I peeked into the narcotics squad's notes, I saw that Stahl was brought in on some kind of a possession charge. It doesn't look like he got a chance to call his attorney. That could mean he was cooperating."

I said, "I think I'm following you. One of your narcotics guys grabbed him, then let him go for no documented reason. Sounds like he might've made a deal, all right." I couldn't help but reach in my pocket and feel the safety-deposit key I had taken from Alton. There were too many leaks in the Newburgh Police Department to let anyone know I had it.

Jeffries was taking a few notes from the computer screen and looked troubled by what he saw.

"Who's the cop that arrested Pete?"

"He was on a temporary duty assignment. I was looking to see if maybe he screwed up some paperwork and that's why they had to release your friend."

"Who was the cop?"

"Mike Tharpe."

CHAPTER 22

THE ORANGE COUNTY jail, where anyone held on charges from Newburgh ended up, was an unimpressive, sprawling structure surrounded by a twelve-foot-high chain-link fence. It was also in the village of Goshen, about thirty-five miles west of Newburgh. That's where my brother had been cooling his heels after his initial bond hearing failed to win his release.

The jailers were clearly breaking my balls by making me wait in one room after another while they said they were getting my brother ready for our visit. I stopped one of them, a tall muscle-head with the name Norton on a tag, and said, "Do you know how frustrating it is to wait this long for a simple visit?"

Norton shrugged and said, "Probably feels just as frustrating as it does for the cops when some smart-ass tries to take over a homicide investigation."

That answered my question for sure.

I glanced through a couple of *Time* magazines that were

all more than three years old and got to know the layout of the facility by studying a map on the wall.

Finally, two jailers led me to a narrow room, about twice the size of a confessional, with a Plexiglas partition. Natty sat on the other side in a simple orange jumpsuit. We had to speak over a closed-circuit telephone. Natty gestured with his hands to let me know that the call could be monitored. That was important information. Especially considering all the shit that had happened to me the last couple of days.

The first thing Natty said was, "How's Katie holding up?"

"It's you I'm worried about."

"I'm fine. Could be better. I know a couple of the guys in my dorm. Since I'm in here on a homicide charge, everyone's keeping their distance."

I said, "I need some answers, Natty." I didn't like how tired he looked. Eyes bloodshot and his usually neat hair hanging down in an oily curl.

Natty showed no emotion as he said, "Go for it."

"Do you know any more details on the big score Pete and Alton made about six weeks ago? Like where the proceeds are or how to get them?" I was hoping the answer was no. That meant he was never involved.

He shrugged. "You've met Alton. He's the first one to tell you how smart he is. He was always bragging about one thing or another, but he'd never tell me anything important." Then he added, "I was sorry to hear he was killed."

"Word travels fast, even in jail."

My brother shook his head and said, "We have TVs in here. It was on the news."

I just shrugged. "Was anything unusual going on with Pete or Alton?"

"Pete was acting a little funny. He's the one that was all excited about something they did, but he didn't give me any details. I have no idea about Alton. We were never close."

"Did Pete have another partner?"

"We all work alone. Most of the time we're competition. Pete just focused on meth, so he and I got along well. Even though I knew him as a kid, he would have never told me the specifics about his business. Not a smart thing to do in our field."

I said, "He talk to anyone a lot the past few weeks?"

"The only person he started to talk to on a regular basis in the last few weeks was a cop."

"A cop? Which cop?"

"The guy who arrested me, Mike Tharpe."

CHAPTER 23

MY GUT WAS telling me that Mike Tharpe had something to do with the murder of Pete Stahl. Whether he had pulled the trigger himself or if there were others involved was still a mystery. I found a coffee shop, not a Starbucks but a mom-and-pop place. I always supported family businesses, because I hated the muted taste of anything that came out of a corporate restaurant. But what I really wanted was a Wi-Fi connection to make my phone that much faster as I signed into my LexisNexis account. My teenage cousin, Bailey Mae, had talked me into getting one so that my private investigation business could run a little smoother. That's how I had found Mrs. Ledbetter's daughter near Philadelphia so easily.

After a few minutes on my smartphone, I found the house where Mike Tharpe lived. Or at least the address where he paid the electric bills. The house was in an area called Little Britain, southwest of the Stewart Airport, a few miles from downtown Newburgh, but far enough away from the chaos to make a cop feel secure when he got home.

It didn't take long to find the comfortable two story on Station Street. It looked like the kind of place where people dreamed about setting up a life. Quiet, safe, and convenient to a bigger city like Newburgh.

The house was dark and I was out of time. I was also running short on common sense and good judgment. Somehow, the idea of breaking into a cop's house didn't even rank as the dumbest thing I had done all week. I'd chased an armed man for the sake of this case, after all.

I took a minute to survey the house from where I had parked up the street. It was completely dark and the next-door neighbors only had a porch light on. If I was going to do something this stupid, now would be the time. I walked casually up the sidewalk, trying to look as natural as possible. People in neighborhoods like this were generally not too suspicious. At least not of a clean-cut guy.

When I turned toward Tharpe's house, I saw the sticker for an alarm system. Often on my paper route, I helped my customers with other problems around their homes. Just quick little jobs to save them from having to pay a professional. One of the most frequent requests was help with alarm systems that the elderly didn't understand well. When I saw Tharpe's sticker for Malloy Security, I knew he'd bought a second-rate system. Malloy was a shitty company that would slap a sensor on your front and back door. Often customers were lucky if they had hooked it up to a power supply at all.

I scooted around to the back door and saw a keypad. This was going to be easier than I expected. I used a trick an electrician showed me when we were working on one of my customers' houses. I pulled my commemorative Navy knife from my pocket, slipped the blade between the house and the keypad, and ripped the plastic contraption right off the wall. Then I crossed the two wires in the back of the box and heard the beep on the inside of the house saying the alarm was no longer active. It never paid to be cheap where security was involved.

The lock on the door was a little more complicated. When you're desperate, though, a few locks can't hold you. I laid my shoulder into the door and it almost came off the frame as it opened up.

I flipped on the light. It was obvious I would never be able to hide the damage to the back door. Now it was all about speed. I bolted up the stairs and rummaged through a few drawers in the bedroom and a little office. I wasn't sure what I was looking for, but I had to find something that would link Tharpe to Pete Stahl.

I worked my way back to the kitchen and had just about tossed the entire house upside down when headlights washed through the living room as a car pulled into the driveway.

I prayed Tharpe would use the front door and not remember if he left the light on or not. The one thing I did know: I was about to get either some answers or a bullet in the head.

CHAPTER 24

I HEARD THE car door and realized my best chance to escape would be to scoot out the back now. But something kept me from doing it. The idea of my brother sitting in jail for Pete Stahl's death kept my feet firmly in the hallway near the kitchen. I had to get to the bottom of this.

I could see the front door over the first few stairs. As it opened, I eased back into a dark nook in the wall that looked like it used to be a linen closet. Like the rest of the house, there hadn't been much renovation there. The door had been taken off the hinges and a few shelves removed. But I felt secure, at least for the moment.

I could barely see the front door as it opened. There was a hesitation as Tharpe stood in the doorway and tried to figure out if he had left the light on in the kitchen. I could see the Marine in him as he surveyed the front room and took a step toward the stairs to get a better view.

My heart was racing as I ran through the options in my head. In that moment, I was a burglar, but if I did much more I'd be considered a home invader. Neither looked good on a résumé. But at least I'd have my brother to talk to in jail.

Tharpe peeked into the kitchen and must've seen the back door busted open. That made him reach with his right hand and draw his service weapon, a Glock semiautomatic. He held it up in his right hand and pointed it up the stairs.

I knew what he was doing. I would've done the same thing. He was listening. He wanted to hear a footstep upstairs or the creaking of a door. He put his back against the wall and let his eyes scan all around the house.

Then I saw my chance. He stepped away from the wall and was about to turn and climb the stairs. I made a decision and acted. That's what the SEALs taught me to do. I stepped from my hiding place and swung my right hand hard, catching him in the side of the head. The blow knocked him off balance and his face hit the side of the stairs as he went down hard.

I immediately grabbed his gun, which had tumbled to the floor. I pulled the magazine and ejected the round left in the chamber. Then I stuck the magazine back into the gun and laid it on the floor near Tharpe's unconscious body. At least he wouldn't be able to pick it up and fire it without racking another round into the chamber.

I rolled Tharpe over to make sure he was breathing and realized I may have been searching in the wrong place. If I had something portable and important, I'd keep it on me. First, I rummaged through his coat pockets, then I felt his front right pocket. At the bottom, securely in place, was a single flat metal key. I pulled it out and immediately recognized it as the same kind of safety-deposit key I took from Alton Beatty. It had the number 68 etched in it.

I felt like I'd solved everything until I thought about it for a minute. How could I prove where I'd found the key? What kind of evidence did I have to implicate the police officer in anything illegal? How would it help my brother? It would be my word against Tharpe's. Although I knew *I* was beyond reproach, I doubt the legal system realized it.

At least, since I wasn't an official police officer, I didn't have to worry about how I obtained evidence or built a case. What I needed were a few more breaks, but finding this key was a good start.

I knew Tharpe couldn't be the third partner. Neither Pete nor Alton would've trusted him. This key had come from Pete, and I was quite certain the beefy police officer had killed my friend for it.

Tharpe started to stir and I took that as my cue to leave. I scooted out the shattered back door and raced to my car down the street. I backed away so I wouldn't have to pass in front of the house. As I reached the end of the street, I could see Tharpe stepping through the front door and standing on his front porch. That son of a bitch was tough.

Maybe all that Marine bullshit about being tougher than everyone else was true.

I tried to make a stealthy getaway, but when you're in a ten-year-old station wagon, trying to get away from a house you just burglarized, that's a tall order.

At least now I had my suspect.

CHAPTER 25

I SAT IN Tina's Plentiful and downed a hamburger with two beers. After the night I'd experienced, I had earned a couple of beers. I had also earned the right to talk to Alicia, but I was disappointed to see she had a number of customers.

It gave me a few minutes to figure out what I was going to do next. I had two keys to the safe-deposit box that held some kind of crazy drug recipe worth a fortune and at least $650,000 in cash. I wanted nothing to do with the contents of the safety-deposit box, but I was trying to see how I might use it to help my brother.

When it was clear Alicia wouldn't be able to sit and chat with me, I decided it was time to catch my mother up on everything that had happened. At least the stuff that wouldn't scare the shit out of her. I intended to avoid the story about chasing a man with a gun or invading a cop's home.

I pulled up in front of my mom's neat brick house. All

the neighbors were home from work and the street and driveways were filled with cars. I rapped on the front door as I poked my head inside and called out, "Mom?"

I stepped into the house and saw my dog, Bart Simpson, on the couch in the front room, wagging his tail at the sight of me. He was comfortable and didn't feel like jumping down to show his affection. I understood that. My mom often kept Bart here at the house if I had to work in the afternoons. She liked the company and so did Bart.

Mom called out, "Bobby, I'm back here."

I cut through the kitchen into the sunken family room and saw she was sitting on the edge of the couch, talking to a visitor at the far end of the couch. As I was about to apologize for interrupting, my mother turned slightly and I saw her visitor. It was Mike Tharpe.

I stood for a moment, speechless. That doesn't happen all that often, but I had to gather my thoughts. When he turned and smiled at me, I noticed his black eye where he'd hit the edge of the stairs. It was a satisfying sight, on a certain level.

Tharpe said, "I was just telling your mom that I think I might have found some evidence that will get your brother out of jail."

"What kind of evidence?" It was clear my mom was buying this bullshit story.

"We think there are two safety-deposit keys that can

open a box with the evidence we need. The problem is the keys have gone missing. I was just about to ask her to call you to come over to help me find them. You know, since you're such a good private investigator and all."

He had more subtlety in him than I thought. But I let a smile spread across my face so he knew I had both keys and understood what he was saying. I waited as it sank in and said, "How would that help? Doesn't the district attorney have to be involved?"

Now my mom jumped in, saying, "Don't cloud the issue, Bobby. He says he can help Natty."

I said, "Mom, he can do a lot of things, but helping Natty is not one of them." I could feel the mood change in the room. Not only did my mom stiffen, but Tharpe realized there was no way to do this quietly.

Tharpe stood up and I realized he was still in the same clothes as at his house. He had known that he needed to find me. He must've seen me drive away from his house. *Damn my big clunker.* I had to get a smaller car.

After my mom stood up like she was going to break up a fight between us, I said, "If you don't think my brother is guilty, then who killed Pete Stahl?"

"Does it really matter?"

"More than you would understand. He was my friend and his family lives here in Marlboro. I can't let something like that go."

Tharpe let out a chuckle, but his eyes didn't show any humor. "That's very noble of you, dropout. But it's a big mistake." He stepped to the side and calmly drew his service weapon, letting it point at the ground. Not too showy, but he got his point across.

It was one thing to threaten me, but no one, and I mean no one, threatens my mom.

CHAPTER 26

A KILLER HAD my mom by the arm and I had never felt so helpless. I had to buy time and engage this creep.

I said, "What's your plan? Kill a fifty-five-year-old nurse to cover a drug deal?"

My mom mumbled, "Fifty-three."

Tharpe said, "No one has to die. Just give me the keys and all is forgotten. If not…" He raised the gun to my mother's head.

Suddenly she realized exactly what was going on and let out a little whimper. This was coming from the toughest woman I had ever known. My stomach flipped. Then I realized Mom didn't look scared, she looked pissed off. Right then, I knew I had to act. This jerk wouldn't forget anything. As soon as he had the keys, my mom and I would both be dead and Natty would spend the rest of his life in jail.

My gun was two blocks away in my own house. Then I realized his gun probably didn't have a bullet in the chamber.

Had he checked his gun after I'd knocked the crap out of him? My guess was that he hadn't.

I raised my hands slowly and said, "Okay, okay. We can work this out."

I tried to calculate the probability of whether he had checked his gun. Was there a round in the chamber? I shook the idea out of my head. Whatever my calculation revealed, I couldn't risk my mom's life on it. I needed Tharpe's full attention on me. I wanted his anger completely focused on me.

I said, "Typical Marine, threatening a woman." I took a tiny step backward and to the side.

Tharpe looked at me and said, "A SEAL dropout is questioning Marine honor?" He lowered the pistol from my mom's head and pointed it in my direction. "You, a goddamn paperboy, think you can cross me."

I took another step back. The gun followed me and he took a step away from my mother. Now my mom was behind him, and I felt emboldened.

Tharpe said, "I should've taken your head off with that crowbar."

I reached up to feel the Band-Aid that was still stuck to my forehead. At least one mystery was solved.

I said, "You're not even smart enough to hold on to the key you stole."

Now the big cop was mad. That meant he wasn't thinking. I pounced on the moment and said, "I took the bullet out of the chamber when I knocked the shit out of you ear-lier." I saw the surprise on his face and knew I had been right.

Then he acted. Quickly. His left hand sprang onto the back of the pistol so he could rack it.

I barreled into him, knocking him back and batting away the pistol before it was operational. We tumbled onto my mom's new laminate floor, and I got a good shot on his chin with a closed fist.

He didn't give up. He hit me with an elbow that made me literally see sparkles. I sprang away from him and to my feet. He rolled to one side and was up quickly as well. I glanced around the floor but had no idea where the gun had gone.

We squared off. All I could think was how much I was going to enjoy this. Tharpe had a lot to answer for, and I was about to exact payment. Then I saw movement behind him. I heard a loud *thunk* and Tharpe dropped to his knees, then lay out flat on the floor.

When I looked up, my mom was holding her heavy cast-iron skillet.

She shook her head and said, "That guy is an asshole."

"Tell me about it."

CHAPTER 27

I HANDCUFFED THARPE behind his back and around the legs of a wooden chair with his own set of cuffs. When he came to, he tried to give us a tough expression, but it's hard to do when you're trussed up like a steer at a rodeo. It had no effect whatsoever.

I pulled a chair close, but not too close. I eased into it so he could see that I'd taken his pistol, which I had found under the TV, and tucked it into my belt. I said, "Don't feel bad. You're not the first victim of my mom's frying pan. She clocked my brother a couple of months ago. I don't think he's right yet. I wish she could back me up on the street sometimes."

Tharpe glared at me as he growled, "You understand the deep shit you're in?"

"You think? Let's call the Ulster County sheriff and let them sort this whole situation out." I pulled my phone from my pocket and started to punch in numbers.

Tharpe said, "Wait."

"Why?"

"Maybe we can help each other."

"I'm listening."

"If I get the box and you let me run, I'll give you a video statement that'll clear your brother."

"You think that'll be enough?"

"Yeah. I'll tell them I did it. I'll confess to killing Pete. And then I'll run for the hills."

"Fine," I said. "I have both keys. Do you have the code?"

That surprised him. He didn't realize I'd figured out the details.

Tharpe said, "I have the number of a throwaway phone that I can text. All I have to do is tell them when to meet us at the bank."

I took the phone from his inside coat pocket, and when he had pointed out the number, I texted, Meet me at the Poughkeepsie bank at 9 AM tomorrow. I looked at Tharpe and said, "Any idea who the silent partner is?"

He shrugged his shoulders. "Pete Stahl and Alton Beatty knew. They never would tell me. It was their insurance."

A minute later a text came back that said, 9 AM tomorrow. Okay.

Tharpe looked at me and said, "I'll make the statement right there in the safety-deposit vault, on video, when I have the contents of the box."

I gave him a hard stare. "Then I'll never see you again?"

Tharpe smiled and said, "No one will."

CHAPTER 28

IT HAD BEEN an anxious night at my mother's house. Keeping a Newburgh detective in custody is a complicated matter. At first my mother insisted on calling the local sheriff's office, but then she realized this was the best way to get Natty off the hook. I had snatched a couple of hours' sleep while my mom kept an eye on the handcuffed Tharpe. Now I found myself with the big Newburgh detective handcuffed in the front seat of my car.

We crossed the Hudson to Poughkeepsie in silence. I had taken a couple of passes in front of the north branch of the First Poughkeepsie Financial Services. I'd seen commercials for the private bank in four locations, but I'd never had a reason to visit it before. It operated like a bank, with a savings-and-loan division, and it provided a whole series of safety deposit and financial transaction options. A one stop shop for drug dealers, money launderers, and divorce attorneys.

I parked in the front lot amid Jaguars and Cadillacs. At

least my sagging station wagon was unique. The bank was a faux-stately one-story building that tried to project an aura of dignified commerce but came up short. The place was used by too many scammers and thugs to ever be dignified.

Knowing the harsh gun laws in New York and not knowing what security was like inside the bank, I made a tough decision. I didn't want a metal detector to get me thrown in jail and ruin my chances of saving Natty, so I hid my gun under the front seat. I was subtle when I slipped it down there and I let Tharpe believe it was still in the pocket of my jacket.

Tharpe had his usual smirk when he said, "Getting nervous?"

"About what? Anything goes wrong and you're the one who's in deep shit."

"What if our partner doesn't show?"

I looked sideways at him and said, "You know something you're not saying?"

"Not a thing."

"Any ideas about who might show up?"

"If your brother wasn't in the can, I'd say him. So it's gotta be some other lowlife dealer. I'll probably recognize him."

We sat in the car for a minute. I checked out the surroundings. Poughkeepsie is a bigger city than either Marlboro or Newburgh and showed signs of growth. There was a completely different vibe here, with new businesses opening and only a few vacancies in the strip malls. A Poughkeep-sie police cruiser passed with two officers in the front seat. It made me remember that technically, I was acting illegally, and I wasn't sure how many people would believe my story about Mike Tharpe being a murderer.

I looked at Tharpe and said, "We're going to wait in the lobby." I patted my pocket where I told him the gun was. "Don't give me a reason to use this. We have an agreement. You make the video statement and I let you take everything in the box. You know I don't want to have anything to do with it anyway."

Tharpe looked at me and said, "And you wait before you tell anyone, so I have a chance to get out of town."

I nodded. "Agreed."

He turned so I could use the key on the handcuffs and free his hands. Then we both eased out of the car, feeling each other out. Tharpe looked tired. It didn't seem like he had any tricks up his sleeve. I let him walk just in front of me as we entered the bank, and I explained to a reception-ist, sitting behind a cramped desk, that we wanted to go to the safety-deposit room after our business partner arrived. The pretty, young receptionist motioned us to a small wait-ing area, where we sat on hard plastic chairs. A velvet rope separated the waiting area from the rest of the lobby, which also served as the entrance to the other sections of the bank.

I looked into the main lobby and evaluated the everyday business the private bank did. There were young mothers with their children and an old couple waiting to speak to a loan officer. Nothing out of the ordinary.

Now I wondered who would show up to meet us. There were too many possibilities to anticipate anything. Tharpe didn't say a word and looked like he was waiting to visit his stockbroker. Every car that pulled into the lot drew my attention.

Then the one car I didn't want to see pulled up. A dark-blue BMW. As I watched out the wide window, I saw Katie Stahl emerge from the car and stroll to the front door of the bank, like she was on a normal errand.

Tharpe smiled and said, "Well, well, well, little miss perfect has a dark secret. It makes me like her that much more."

She hesitated for a moment in the parking lot, staring at us through the window, then regained her composure.

And my heart broke a little bit.

CHAPTER 29

BY THE LOOK on Katie's face, she didn't know who she was going to meet, either. She stood at the edge of the waiting area, right in front of us, brown leather car coat with a fur trim and red Aldo purse draped over her shoulder. Her blond hair hung down her back in a loose ponytail. She wore the same black running shoes my mom did at the hospital. She must've come directly from work.

It felt like the three of us were in an Old West standoff, silently assessing one another as the sounds of normal bank business drifted across the tile floor.

I scanned the tellers behind us. There were no visible security guards and no one was paying any attention to our little moment in the corner.

Katie's eyes cut to Tharpe.

I said quickly, "He's not here in an official capacity."

Tharpe let out a cough and muttered, "That's an understatement."

Katie ignored him, turned to me, and said, "Hello, Mitchum. I didn't expect to see you here."

"Who did you expect to see?"

She gave Tharpe a nasty glance and said, "I don't know. But he doesn't surprise me at all."

I could've explained my involvement to her, but right now I needed this to go quickly. Besides, she didn't deserve to know exactly what was going on.

"Do you have the code?" I asked, hoping she was some kind of a pawn.

She nodded and said, "Do you still intend to split it evenly?"

Tharpe mumbled, "Not as evenly as any previous agreement."

I cut in. "We'll work it out. The only thing I want is for Natty to be released." I just needed Tharpe's statement. After that, these two could negotiate.

Katie considered this. When she nodded, I realized there was no way she'd been more than just a pawn. That didn't just break my heart, it pissed me off.

The three of us walked down the long hallway, past the armed security guard, and met an attendant who led us down another long hallway to the room that held box number 68. The building was designed like a maze, and I stood in the center of it with a guy I hated and a woman who had tricked my whole family. Great. Just another Wednesday in upstate New York.

The attendant, a thin man in his forties with a Boston accent, said, "Who has the code?"

Katie stepped up and faced the keypad on the side of the closed door. She pulled a small piece of paper from her purse and punched in the five-digit code.

The tumblers in the door turned and it popped open.

The attendant looked at me as if I was in charge and said, "Number 68 is on the top row in the corner. There's a table and two chairs. Would you like me to find another chair?"

I shook my head.

He smiled and said, "I'll be right down the hall if you need anything at all."

The three of us entered the room slowly. It was the size of a bedroom. Maybe ten by twelve feet. Up against three of the walls there were boxes of different sizes. Everything was gray. The boxes in the wall, the door. Even the ceiling was a lighter shade of gray. There was no natural light, just a sleek tract of soft LED lights. Ten minutes in here would drive anyone crazy.

I pulled out both keys from my front pocket. Before I inserted them into the round locks on the box, I looked at Tharpe and said, "Let's get your video statement first."

He hesitated, so I let my hand slip inside my pocket where he thought I was holding a gun. He nodded and sat down in one of the two chairs at the table in the center of the room.

I quickly recorded his statement, and when I looked up, Katie was at the far end of the room, holding a gun on both of us.

CHAPTER 30

IT WAS HARD to take my eyes off the gun in Katie Stahl's hand. She clearly had no regard for the gun laws of New York. There was a little tremor in the barrel, but overall she seemed calm and confident. Always bad news for the person facing the gun.

The sea of gray and soft lighting wasn't helpful at all. I felt like I was stuck in a cavern, surrounded by a building.

She looked at me and said, "I'm not enjoying this."

I said, "If it makes you feel any better, neither am I." I tried to read Katie's next move. I'd wait for my chance.

I turned my attention to the box. Mike Tharpe stood to my right and I knew a guy like him had to be calculating the odds of escape. He'd already lost his old life. He'd never be a cop again. Now it looked like he was losing his new life as well. I didn't want him to do anything desperate.

I slowly turned both keys in the lock at the same time. Once they turned all the way to the left, the door unlatched and I pulled it open. I reached inside and pulled out a safety-deposit box that was about the size of a recycling bin. With the lid closed it looked like a big, gray building block.

I plopped it down onto the table. Tharpe was eyeing it like a wolf stalking a sheep. I stepped back to the wall and said to Katie, "You open it." I thought I might trick her into a mistake. Maybe tie up her hands for a second. But I had no such luck.

She pointed the semiautomatic pistol at Tharpe and said, "Let him do it." With her other hand, she gave him a piece of paper with the code written on it. Katie was in control and appeared ready to shoot if she had to. This wasn't how I imagined a pretty occupational therapist would behave.

Tharpe moved forward, cutting his eyes toward me. When he focused on the box, he paused. Then he unlatched the front and lifted the lid like it was the Ark of the Covenant. We all looked on in silence.

There was a leather-bound notepad and a cloth sack. Tharpe picked up the notepad and thumbed through it quickly. Nothing but page after page of instructions and formulas.

He set the book on the table. Then he pulled the cloth sack from the box. It was fairly large, about the size of a kitchen garbage bag. When he pulled open the drawstring, all I could see as I peered over his shoulder was cash. Bundles of hundred-dollar bills. Lots of bundles. Bundles of dreams.

I had never seen that much money. I would probably never make that much money in my entire life. It annoyed me. How could people have that kind of cash? Suddenly I didn't like the idea of Tharpe taking it. It seemed wrong, no matter what deal we had made earlier.

Katie read his intentions, too. She said, "This was everything Pete worked for. He gave his life for it. I can't let it be stolen. Don't make me shoot you."

I noticed Tharpe out of the corner of my eye. He was trying to be subtle and get my attention. As Katie gazed into the box, he used two fingers to make a gun sign. Then I realized he thought I really had a gun in my jacket and he wanted me to shoot her. Even if I was armed, I wasn't going to shoot Katie over this garbage in the box. It wasn't worth it.

I stayed where I was and raised my hands slightly. Part of it was a show of surrender to Katie, but when I turned, my jacket pulled tight and Tharpe saw that I didn't have a gun.

And that's when he decided to make his move.

CHAPTER 31

THARPE LURCHED FORWARD, fast. Faster than I thought a guy his size could. He slapped Katie's hand to one side, then reached across to grab the gun. It slipped out of both of their hands, bounced off the table, and clattered onto the floor. That's when things got really rough inside the tiny vault.

I dove for the gun as Tharpe tumbled over the table to get it. We met on the hard tile floor. Each of us had a hand on the gun. We tried to find the right leverage to pry it from the other man's hands. We rolled on the floor, bumping into the boxes in the wall and the legs of the table. Each bruise made me angrier and angrier.

I was hoping Katie would help me. All she had to do was push the heavy box off the table onto Tharpe's face. Instead, she stepped forward and started to collect the contents of the box for herself. I managed to gain a hold of the gun and struggled to my feet as Tharpe was hanging on as hard as he could.

He had a weight advantage on me and used it well. He

twisted hard and jerked me into the wall of safety-deposit boxes. But no Marine was going to get the better of me. I raised my knee and caught him hard in the abdomen, driving him back. Then his fingers tangled in mine near the gun and he pulled it back before smacking it against my temple.

I quickly regained my bearings, and as soon as I did, the gun discharged. In the enclosed space it was like being next to a thunderclap. My brain scrambled for a second.

I let go with my left hand and threw a punch hard into his face. He staggered back.

The smell of the gunpowder hung in the smoky air and stung my eyes.

That was when I saw Katie. On the ground. The blood pumping out of a wound in her chest. I couldn't help myself, and let go of the gun. I dropped to my knee to try and stop the blood pumping out through the hole in her leather jacket. It pooled on her chest.

Tharpe wasted no time grabbing the gun, sack of money, and notebook. He slipped out of the room instantly.

Katie tried to say something. It might've been "I'm sorry," but maybe I was imagining it. No real sound came out. Within moments, I felt her body go still underneath my hand and I knew she was dead.

I heard shouting in the hallway as Tharpe tried to get past the security guard. That's when a shot was fired.

This plan had gone completely to shit.

CHAPTER 32

SURROUNDED BY THE gray walls, I felt my anger rise. I didn't care if Katie Stahl was the mastermind or criminal conspirator. Someone else was going to pay for all of this shit. Right now, the only target I saw was Mike Tharpe.

I stood up and took one more look at poor Katie. Then I noticed the piece of paper with the room code written on it next to her. I plucked it off the floor and raced out of the small room.

I crouched just outside of the door to figure out the direction in which Tharpe had fled. The maze of hallways made it difficult. I could hear people screaming. Then I heard gunshots around the corner toward the front of the bank.

I sprinted down the long hallway, dodging the body of the murdered guard. As I got closer, I could hear the chaos. In the lobby, a young mother clutched her baby and ran for cover. An elderly man fell and just stayed on the tile, reaching up uselessly, like a turtle on its back. Customers and tellers alike were scrambling past him and shouting. Security had spread around the perimeter of the room.

When I turned to my right, I immediately saw Tharpe crouched behind a heavy planter with leafy branches spreading out above him. This hallway led to the waiting area where we had come from.

Tharpe leaned out from behind the planter and took a potshot at a security guard twenty feet away. Tharpe intended to flee out the front, but this guy held his ground. Good for him.

The security guard was using a column as cover and he had the advantage of time on his side. The police would arrive before long. All he had to do was keep Tharpe behind the planter.

I crept toward Tharpe in his blind spot. When I was about a dozen feet behind him, I tried to signal the security guard by waving my arm. The last thing I wanted was to catch one of his bullets by mistake. Or on purpose, if he thought I was Tharpe's partner.

The guard looked like a deer in the headlights. I had to risk the chance that he saw me.

I made my move.

CHAPTER 33

I JUST DOVE in. Like I was playing football in school. I led with my shoulder. Tharpe made a *humph* sound as I drove him into the planter.

I wrapped both hands around his right wrist to keep him from pointing the pistol in my direction. I jerked him away from the planter, expecting the guard to give me some sort of support. I didn't care if he shot Tharpe while I had him in the open. Instead, I was in dogfight mode. The SEAL mentality was to never lose. This time I wanted to make the loser pay.

I jerked Tharpe closer and head-butted him in the nose. He staggered back, blood already dripping from his nostrils. He managed to hold on to the gun. He even squeezed off a round that kept the security guard behind the pillar.

I stole a peek at the lobby and saw that it was still in chaos. A woman screamed and ran for the front door. I hoped others would follow her.

I focused on Tharpe again and used my legs to drive him

into the wall. He crashed hard. The whole building seemed to shake.

Then I twisted and used my body's leverage to snap his right wrist. He let out a grunt of pain as the bones broke. I could hear them as well as feel them shatter under my hands. The gun dropped onto the tile floor. I kicked it hard with my left foot as if it were a soccer ball. It spun across the floor. I threw an elbow into Tharpe's jaw and felt it break under the pressure. The big cop stayed on his feet. Incredible.

He was done. I had the upper hand, but this was the best therapy I could imagine. I wound up my right arm and balled my hand into a fist. Tharpe didn't even know what was coming his way. Then I heard someone shout, "Police! Don't move!"

I looked to my left and saw two uniformed Poughkeepsie cops with their service weapons drawn and pointed at me. They were both young. A blond woman, who couldn't have stood at more than five foot one, and a lanky guy with a military haircut. His pistol clearly shook in his hand.

The security guard pointed at me and said, "That guy stopped the gunman."

That made the cops focus their attention on Tharpe. Then I delivered my punch. It was a wild haymaker that felt like it came from across the Hudson and landed squarely on Tharpe's nose. He stumbled back and hit the wall again.

This time he fell to the ground. That's when I gave him a good, solid kick in the ribs. He grunted and blood poured out of his shattered nose as if it were a garden hose.

The tall cop stepped forward and yelled, "Cut that shit out. Now."

I was already in a stance to kick Tharpe again when I looked over at the cop. He could see I had nothing in my hands and I was no lethal threat. At least not to him. I winked and threw my kick anyway. Tharpe made another satisfying grunt as I felt one of his ribs crack beneath my foot.

I immediately held up both hands and stepped back, mumbling, "Sorry, Officer."

The young patrolman dropped to his knee and started to search Tharpe. The other cop kept her gun trained on me. She had more tactical sense than her partner and didn't step forward.

The cop cuffed Tharpe behind his back, then stood up to face me. He was holding Tharpe's ID case with the Newburgh detective's badge on the outside.

He said, "What the hell is this?"

"That's something he doesn't deserve to carry."

CHAPTER 34

THREE HOURS LATER, I found myself back in Newburgh. I tried to process everything that had happened. The Poughkeepsie police had a lot of questions. They weren't particularly happy with me. There wasn't much they could do. It was a mess and there was no chance to spin it in a positive way. A cop had gone bad, and because of him, there were bodies in both Newburgh and Poughkeepsie.

I didn't knock when I entered the law office of Lise Mendez. There had been some vague reports on the news from Poughkeepsie. I figured she didn't have any of the details yet.

She didn't seem surprised to see me as I stood in her door. She looked up from her desk and gave me one of those dazzling smiles. "Hello, Mitchum. What are you doing here?"

"I just came from Poughkeepsie."

"What's going on in Poughkeepsie?"

"You can try and play this cool, but I think we're past that."

She elected to remain silent.

"I know you sent Katie Stahl to collect the money."

"I have no idea what…"

"Save it." I held up the piece of paper that Katie used to read the code for the safety-deposit-box room. It was a blue Post-it note with the logo across the top that said *Adirondacks are not only chairs.*

Lise froze in place.

"When I saw this Post-it with the security code, it took me a minute to remember where I'd seen this logo before." I started walking across the room, slowly.

Lise didn't move. She followed me with her eyes.

I said, "You were the perfect partner for drug dealers. If the cops ever had questions, you could've claimed attorney–client privilege. And Pete trusted you." I stopped at her desk. I saw the Post-it pad with the same logo near her pen in the corner of her desk.

I stared at her, waiting for some sort of response.

She finally said, "That's hardly a basis for an indictment, let alone a conviction."

"Not by itself. Phone records will help. Maybe your handwriting on the pad. Who knows. Good cops can be persistent."

There was no panic in her voice when she said, "I suppose the money is still at the bank."

Now it was my turn to keep quiet.

She said, "What can we do?"

"You think you can make some kind of deal?" I took a step back so I wouldn't be tempted. "It's a great idea. Make Katie do the dirty work. You get a big wad of cash and get to remain Newburgh's top criminal defense attorney. Pretty sweet deal."

Then the front door opened and Sergeant Bill Jeffries walked in with three other Newburgh police officers. One detective already had handcuffs ready.

I looked at Lise and said, "The problem is there are still a lot of good cops in Newburgh. For your sake, let's hope there's at least one other good attorney."

CHAPTER 35

THE GRAY CLOUDS that hung low in the sky over Woodlawn Cemetery in New Windsor matched my mood exactly. The cold crept into my bones as I stood next to my brother. The crowd of friends and family listened to a Presbyterian minister say a few words over Katie Stahl's grave. Her family wanted nothing to do with Natty and that suited him fine.

It had been six days since the "shootout in Poughkeepsie," as the newspapers called it. Katie had been listed as a victim of a cop gone bad. That was better than I had hoped she'd be represented. The media tended to focus on the more sensational aspects of a case like this, so naturally, they wanted to talk about the corrupt cop in this sting. That caught people's attention. Not the fact that other cops jumped to make the case against Mike Tharpe and set things right as soon as they found out about it. All anyone talked about was a single bad apple.

If I was mentioned in any story, it was always as someone

trying to help his brother who'd been charged with a murder. I was worried someone would use the phrase "private investigator," and I'd have to explain myself to the New York Department of Business and Professional Regulation. There may not have been a specific charge about impersonating a private investigator, but I'm sure someone would have charged me a decent fine, and my days of helping the residents of Marlboro might be over.

Some of the news stories liked to show photos of Lise Mendez and talk about the pretty attorney who'd been involved in a drug conspiracy. She was now being held without bond on a slew of charges.

As for Mike Tharpe, he pled guilty to the murders of Alton Beatty and Katie Stahl, after I'd handed in his confession tape for Pete's murder. That would help reduce his sentence, but he'd still be away for a long time.

After the service, we walked to Natty's leased red Chevy Camaro with its extra-wide twenty-two-inch rear wheels. It looked like something a seventeen-year-old would drive.

As I slipped into the passenger seat I said, "You know, I could've driven."

Natty let out a short laugh and said, "I can't be seen in a car like yours. Sorry, no offense."

We drove through Newburgh on 9W in silence. I noticed Natty was pushing it and we were cruising at over seventy.

I said, "We're going a little fast, aren't we?"

"I thought you were a fake private investigator, not a fake cop."

I chuckled and mumbled, "Funny."

Natty pushed the sleek car a little harder and took it up over eighty as we left Balmville. Then he said, "I really did love her."

It was the first time he'd talked about Katie since he'd gotten out of jail the day after she was killed.

I said, "I know. She was a great girl. She just got caught up in something she didn't understand."

"It makes me think about my profession and lifestyle. I never knew what it was like to lose something as precious as Katie."

I did know, but I kept quiet. I liked seeing my brother grow up right in front of me, even if it was a dozen years later than everyone else usually did.

Natty said, "Who would've thought that after all these years, you'd be the one to understand what I'm going through? You're the person I can count on the most."

I shrugged and said, "I figured I'd have to bail you out of trouble sooner or later."

Now Natty smiled and said, "You're an asshole, but I love you."

"I love you, too." Then the car hit ninety and I added, "Asshole."

ABOUT THE AUTHORS

James Patterson has written more bestsellers and created more enduring fictional characters than any other novelist writing today. He lives in Florida with his family.

James O. Born is an award-winning crime and science-fiction novelist as well as a career law enforcement agent. A native Floridian, he still lives in the Sunshine State.

"HAVE YOU SEEN MY COUSIN...ALIVE?"

Rejected by the Navy SEALs, Mitchum is content to be his small town's unofficial private eye, until his beloved fourteen-year-old cousin is abducted. Now he'll call on every lethal skill to track her down—but nothing is what it seems....

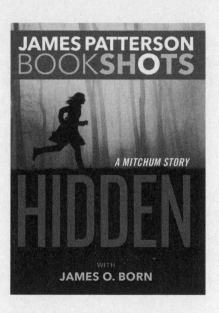

Read the first book in the Mitchum series, the suspenseful shocker *Hidden,* available only from

BOOK**SHOTS**

WHO IS KILLING NEW YORK'S MOST BEAUTIFUL WOMEN IN THE CITY'S FINEST STORES?

Gorgeous women are dropping dead at upscale department stores in New York City. Detective Luc Moncrief and Detective Katherine Burke are close to solving the mystery, but looks can be deceiving....

Read the shocking finale to the French detective trilogy, *French Twist,* available only from

HARRY POSEHN IS THE BEST DAD, THE BEST HUSBAND... WELL, *MAYBE NOT.*

Detective Teaghan Beaumont is getting closer and closer to discovering the truth about Harry Posehn. But there's a twist that she—and you, dear reader—will never see coming.

Can Beaumont catch him before it's too late? Read *The House Husband,* **available only from**

BOOKSHOTS

HER HUSBAND HAS A TERRIBLE SECRET....

Miranda Cooper's life takes a terrifying turn when an SUV deliberately runs her family's car off a desolate Arizona road. With her husband badly wounded, she must run for help alone as his cryptic parting words echo in her head: "Be careful who you trust."

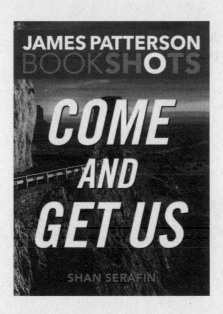

Read the heart-pounding thriller, *Come and Get Us*, available now from

BOOKSHOTS

GOD SAVE THE QUEEN—ONLY PRIVATE CAN SAVE THE ROYAL FAMILY.

Private is the most elite detective agency in the world. But when kidnappers threaten to execute a royal family member in front of the Queen, Jack Morgan and his team have just twenty-four hours to stop them. Or heads will roll…literally.

Read the brand-new addition to the Private series, *Private: The Royals,* **available now only from**

IS HARRIET BLUE AS TALENTED A DETECTIVE AS LINDSAY BOXER?

Harriet Blue, the most single-minded detective since Lindsay Boxer, won't rest until she stops a savage killer targeting female university students. But new clues point to a more chilling predator than she could ever have imagined....

**Will Harriet solve the case before time runs out?
Read *Black & Blue*, available only from**

BOOKSHOTS

THE GREATEST STORY IN MODERN HISTORY HAS A NEW CHAPTER....

Posing as newlyweds, two ruthless thieves board the *Titanic* to rob its well-heeled passengers. But an even more shocking plan is afoot—a sensational scheme that could alter the fate of the world's most famous ship.

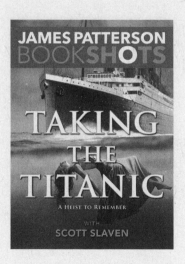

The world's most famous ship lives again in this thrilling tale, *Taking the Titanic,* available only from

Looking to Fall in Love in Just One Night?

Introducing BookShots Flames:

Original romances presented by James Patterson that fit into your busy life.

Featuring Love Stories by:

New York Times bestselling author Jen McLaughlin

New York Times bestselling author Samantha Towle

New York Times bestselling author Sabrina York

USA Today bestselling author Erin Knightley

Elizabeth Hayley

Jessica Linden

Codi Gary

Laurie Horowitz

…and many others!

Available only from

HE'S WORTH MILLIONS…
BUT HE'S WORTHLESS WITHOUT HER.

Siobhan Dempsey came to New York with a purpose: she wants to become a successful artist. But then she meets tech billionaire Derick Miller, who takes her breath away. And though Siobhan's body comes alive at his touch, their relationship has been a roller-coaster ride.

Are they meant to be together?

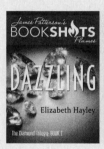  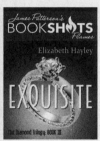

Read the steamy Diamond Trilogy books:

Dazzling, The Diamond Trilogy: Book I

Radiant, The Diamond Trilogy: Book II

Exquisite, The Diamond Trilogy: Book III

Available only from

THE McCULLAGH INN IS NOW OPEN FOR WEDDINGS.

Jeremy Holland is exactly what Chelsea O'Kane wants in a man. After he proposes, she's ecstatic to host their wedding at the inn they built together. But it isn't long before secrets from Chelsea's past refuse to stay buried, and they could ruin everything....

Read the heart-stopping love story, *A Wedding in Maine,* available only from

Also check out
The McCullagh Inn in Maine.